Earthbound Bones

by Regina Welling

Earthbound Bones

ISBN-978-1530857883
ISBN-1530857880

Cover art and interior design by:
L. Vryhof

www.reginawelling.com

First Edition
Printed in the U.S.A.

Table of Contents

Prologue...5
Chapter One..9
Chapter Two 27
Chapter Three 37
Chapter Four..47
Chapter Five 55
Chapter Six 67
Chapter Seven..77
Chapter Eight...89
Chapter Nine..99
Chapter Ten 115
Chapter Eleven 125
Chapter Twelve 143
Chapter Thirteen 149
Chapter Fourteen 163
Chapter Fifteen 171
Chapter Sixteen 177
Chapter Seventeen 181
Chapter Eighteen 189
Chapter Nineteen 193
Chapter Twenty 197

Prologue

Thirty Years Ago

One hand on the wheel, the other clutching an ice cold beer, condensation slick on the can—he raised a toast to the three jerks who ruined the last fishing trip they'd ever take together. The half hour between sunset and night dropped the flat light of dusk over the hood of the car he'd cobbled together from junkyard rejects. All she needed was a coat of paint.

The sharp smell of yeast and hops hit his nose mere seconds before he noticed the damp spreading over his crotch. Much, much later he would swear he only took his eyes off the road for half a second to tend to his beer-soaked Levis.

Four teenagers dodging school for one last fishing trip on the lake, a campfire, and a case of Pabst Blue Ribbon. Those were the parts of that day he preferred to remember.

Not the trees coming at him when he looked up. Not the desperate wrench of the wheel to get back in his own lane. Not the sickening thud, the crunch, or the heart-stopping panic taking him from totally buzzed to completely sober. Not the round white face, the fear-filled eyes, or the bright smear of blood. Not coming home muddy and tired. Those memories he did his best to shove into the darkest recesses of his mind, where the light of memory would have to strain to find them.

The past was the past. Everything and everyone in it needed to stay buried. He would make sure it did. No matter what. He couldn't handle what would happen if it didn't.

Galmadriel

Angels never sleep—which is why waking up disoriented and draped over a pile of bodies meant something had gone terribly, terribly wrong.

Light pounded through my slitted eye, forcing me to close it until my brain could adjust to the onslaught.

Somewhere nearby, a clock ticked away endless seconds while I tried to remember who I was, where I was, and what had happened to me. The buzzing mist in my head amplified the noise from a soft click to an echoing boom. I counted ten, then fifteen seconds before the first memory came rushing back.

My name is Galmadriel. I am—or at least I was—a guardian angel. As if unlocking a door, that knowledge unleashed a literal eternity of memories: watching over my charges; crying for them when they needed to walk through the dark in order to find the light; feeling gutted for those who refused my help, and then devastated for the one I had failed.

Once the memories came back, my mind wouldn't stop replaying them. The whirling circle closing in around us. The scream ripped from the hell-bound Earthwalker. The mortals who, without hesitation, risked all. The backlash that dragged Kat's soul away before her time, and the desperate race to get it back. The final moment when I had either been thrown out of Heaven or fallen from grace. It had happened so quickly I couldn't tell exactly which. Not that it mattered, the end result was the same.

Breaking rules—even for the best of reasons—might have cost me everything: my home; my status as a guardian angel; even my immortality. All of it gone; given up to save two humans from my own folly.

The mortals. I needed to get up and check on them.

Adrenaline coursed through my veins with a jolt that forced my aching body into a sitting position. A soft whine sounded from somewhere behind me, but I dared not turn my head when even the slightest movement spun the world and made me wobble.

Another whine accompanied a flutter of motion while I waited, first for the whirling to stop, and then for my eyes to clear. I turned my head to meet Lola's liquid brown gaze. What was it about boxer dogs that made them look sad even when their tails were wagging? Before I could turn my head again, she treated me to a swipe of her tongue, and while it was softer and warmer than I would have expected, the experience was not one I wanted to repeat.

I blinked away the last of the fog to bring the sprawl of bodies into sharp focus. A gusting sigh escaped my lips at the sight before me. All eight of the humans breathed rhythmically. They lived. Relief ebbed the adrenaline like a calming balm over a bee sting. Three deep breaths saw it leaving my system, and my thrumming heart began to slow.

In a moment, they would start to stir. There would be questions I didn't want to answer—probably couldn't answer, come to that. We had banished an Earthwalker—a malevolent spirit—from a man possessed. A victory to be sure. One worth celebrating if not for what happened next. My hubris allowed Kat's spirit to cross over while her body still lived. To get her back I broke a cardinal rule by sending Zack across to retrieve her.

Amethyst, the aura reader, led the rest of the humans in anchoring the living side, while the two ghosts helped me sustain the connection to spirit. Holding the bridge in place had proved too much for us and when it let go, I went along with it. Dragged or tossed out of heaven and into this mortal body. All I remembered was the endless sensation of falling.

These were good, caring people. All eight of them with an endless capacity for love. Still, feeling unable to cope with their sympathy, I sneaked out of the house with my head held low to avoid the possibility of seeing my altered shadow. If there was one thing I was still sure of, it was this: fallen angels always lose their wings.

A shaft of sunlight slashed across eyes I mistakenly thought had adjusted to the glare. Not so, I decided, as my temple throbbed straight past ache to pounding, screaming pain. This flesh and bone body seemed so small, so frail, so diminished, so alien.

I could feel it dying around me.

Without thinking, I reached for the power of my grace and willed myself as far from there as I could get. The familiar wash of energy whispered over skin sensitized by its first true taste of wind and everything went gray for the second time that day.

Chapter One

One minute everything was fine; the next, Pam Allen's heart launched into her throat. She stomped her foot on the imaginary passenger-side brake of her food truck. The woman standing in the middle of the road had come from out of nowhere.

Eyes painfully wide and quivering hands pressed to her cheeks, Pam sent a desperate prayer heavenward. It would take either a miracle or divine intervention to stop the truck in time. Seconds turned in on themselves and stretched out like molasses crawling across snow, while driver Hamlin Paine fought to keep control as the tires broke free from the surface of the road. Saucer-sized eyes filled with terror, his hands whipped the wheel to steer into the skid, and he used both feet to pump the brake.

***

Everything went from gray, to living color, to heart-slamming panic in a split second. Helpless, she watched the flat-fronted truck with images of food painted all over it hurtle toward her. Out of habit formed over an eternity, the former angel raised one hand in a gesture no longer infused with power, and whispered, *stop*. Nothing happened—not a fizzle or a spark. The well of pure energy always available to her had become clogged with humanity.

On her first day of being human, Galmadriel was about to die.

Well beyond the ability to form a coherent thought, Galmadriel turned to instinct. She set aside all memory of the fall that had turned her human, and just remembered what it felt like to be an angel. Desperate need and an eternity of ingrained habit imbued Galmadriel's hand with a portion of the power she had once possessed. Loudly and firmly, she repeated the command for the vehicle to stop.

Later, Pam would swear she saw the outline of wings unfolding to shadow the woman's face. Hamlin would argue that a flare of white light had nearly blinded him. At the last second, with time moving at a snail's pace, Galmadriel watched both of them close their eyes and wait for the telltale thump. Her heart hammered so hard she expected it to break through her chest, and she heard screaming long before she realized the voice echoing in her ears was her own.

The flash of energy shooting through her felt nothing like as strong as she was used to commanding; but it was there. All she could do now was wait for the impact.

It never came.

When Galmadriel opened her eyes again—they had fluttered shut on their own—the truck sat motionless, its bumper a fraction of an inch away from her knees, and the windshield nearly pressed against her face.

Lifting one shaky hand, she pushed back the flaming auburn hair that tumbled across her shoulders and cascaded down her back in a tangled mass of bedraggled curls. Beads of sweat pearling on her brow took on an icy chill, and her knees wobbled. Start to finish, the incident had taken less than half a minute. It seemed longer.

"Did you see that? Where did she come from?" Hamlin shouted to Pam right before he swore a streak of language that would have turned a sailor pale. Two sets of trembling hands yanked door handles and the pair of them spilled out onto the pavement.

"Where did you…" Those were the last words Galmadriel heard before a loud buzzing swamped her and the world narrowed to a tiny point of light. Hamlin's lightning fast reflexes kept her from hitting the ground with a thud.

"We didn't hit her, did we? It happened so fast." Galmadriel could still hear his voice faintly fading in and out through the humming in her head, and she felt his shoulders bunch as he lowered her to the ground.

"I don't think so. I think she's just scared. Shocky." Pam opened the door, grabbed an unused jacket from behind the seat, and rolled it up. "If you can hear me, I'm just going to elevate your feet." Her movements were sure and efficient. "Ham, go get me a damp towel, please. Hurry."

In a moment he was back. "Is she okay?"

"She's coming around. We'll know more in a minute." Pam spoke in a soothing voice, calm now the crisis was over, her hands rock steady.

After a few shallow breaths, Galmadriel made an effort to relax, then opened her eyes and tried to sit up. "No, just rest there until you get your breath back." Pam laid a gentle but firm hand on Galmadriel's shoulder to push her back down into a prone position.

"I am fine. Please let me up." The words, though quietly spoken came out like a command from on high. Hamlin jerked at the force of them, torn between helping and a healthy reticence for touching a stranger. It was too late, anyway. Galmadriel had already regained her feet. Her new body felt lighter and more agile than expected, given its height.

"What's your name?" Hamlin asked. A simple question; and yet, how could she answer without telling a lie or freaking him out? The words *I am the angel Galmadriel* refused to pass her lips. Probably due to an instinctual need for self-preservation.

Even providing such minor information as her name seemed unwise until she had a better idea of what had brought her to the middle of who-knows-where. In aiming for her home on the other side, there was no doubt she had missed the mark. Completely.

"What happened?" She stalled for time.

"My name is Pam Allen, and I'm the owner of this rolling monstrosity. This," she pointed to the man with her, "is Hamlin Paine. You came out of nowhere and we almost hit you with the truck. Ham barely got it stopped in time."

"Honestly, I'm not sure how I managed it. It was like some force field stood between you and certain death. It was a miracle." Hamlin's voice sounded strained.

At the word miracle, every drop of blood drained out of Galmadriel's face. She shivered at the chill seeping into her bones, though the coolness was not the real reason for her reaction. How could she have been given a miracle after everything that had happened, after being kicked out of heaven?

"Come on," Pam said, "Let's get out of the sun; it's cooler in the truck. Is there someplace we can take you?"

Another question with no viable answer; the silence spun out. Galmadriel avoided Pam's searching gaze, but followed the other woman willingly into the truck. Until she could get her bearings, she had no other recourse.

Hamlin turned toward Pam with questioning eyes and a quirked eyebrow and mouthed, "What now?" She answered with a slight twitch of her shoulders and mouthed back, "No idea."

Now that the initial shock had worn off, Hamlin glanced pointedly at his watch. Galmadriel took his action to mean he was anxious to get on with his day. These two people had been on the way to somewhere before she had so inconveniently dropped in on them. Pam confirmed this by saying, "We were on our way back to town to restock the truck after the morning run. Where can we drop you? Are you visiting friends in the area?"

"No, I am here because..." When she took a moment to think about it, Galmadriel had no idea why I was here.

Turning in her seat, she cast an assessing eye on Pam. What she saw was a woman in her early middle years—a short cap of medium brown hair curled up where it feathered around her ears and framed a pair of lively green eyes. Those eyes currently carried a wary expression. Reading the contours of Pam's face, Galmadriel saw lines of tension around her mouth; lines deeply grooved enough to speak of a tragedy somewhere in the woman's past. In contrast, marks of laughter also crinkled near her eyes, which told Galmadriel Pam was a woman who tried not to dwell on the harder times. Trustworthy, stalwart and true—these were words her instinct said would describe Pam perfectly.

Picking her words carefully, Galmadriel attempted to skirt the more fantastic elements of her story. "I...something has happened to me, and for reasons I cannot explain, I have nowhere to go." Over an eternity of existence, Galmadriel had never felt disconnected from home. Now she was alone and lost.

As if something about her compelled him to offer assistance, Hamlin spoke up, "You can stay with me." Pam later admitted that in the moment, she had felt a similar urge to offer sanctuary but, being a bit more experienced in life, had managed to stop herself before blurting out an offer of help. In her experience, people who fell for a sob story were the ones left crying in the end.

"Thank you for your kindness." Tempting as Hamlin's offer was, Galmadriel felt powerfully drawn to Pam—tuned in to her in much the same way as with her former charges. Something inside Pam was broken. She needed Galmadriel's help almost as much as the former angel needed hers.

With the adrenaline ebbing, Galmadriel began to take in more of her surroundings. It came as a bit of a shock when she glanced out the window expecting to see the gray and brown tones of late March and, instead, saw a vista of gently undulating, daisy-studded grass. She must have lost two, maybe three months in what had felt like the blink of an eye. Where had she been all that time?

Slumping back in the seat, Galmadriel ran back over the debacle that had led her here. None of her actions at the bridge were sanctioned by the collective that governed over guardian angel activities. The powers that be would never have let her attempt such a thing had they known. The plan was reckless and brilliant; too bad she hadn't quite pulled it off.

Even knowing she would have to explain her choices to her superiors and probably pay penance, Galmadriel had intended to use the all's-well-that-ends-well defense. Unfortunately, she never got the chance. Instead, the bridge's moorings failed, and in the ensuing chaos, she fell. Not the kind of fall where you get up, nurse a skinned knee and get back on the horse—the kind where everyone back home, if they spoke of her at all, it would be in hushed tones and using the term *fallen angel*.

Fast forward to now and here she was: worried about turning evil, missing weeks of time, stuck inside a human body, and unable to go home. Definitely not an ends-well situation.

And to top it all off, she had to pee.

***

Spending a millennium as a guardian angel had taught Galmadriel everything she thought she needed to know about life on earth. Odd customs, strange habits, and societal norms all fell within the scope of her knowledge. However, an hour walking in human shoes proved knowing a thing and living it were two entirely different prospects.

Logically, she knew she should focus on long-term goals of finding shelter and a means of financial support. Too bad her flesh and bone body was all about the short term problems. Unless she was mistaken, the gnawing sensation in her gut meant finding food was number one with a bullet on her priority list.

There are no coincidences; any angel will tell you that. Her glance fell on the Help Wanted sign propped in the truck's window, and she remembered the business name emblazoned across the side of the truck: Just Desserts. Dessert was food, right?

Two birds, one stone.

"I would like to help." At Pam's blank look, Galmadriel gestured toward the sign. A slight upward twitch of one brow signaled Pam's surprise.

"Do you have any experience?"

"Not as such, but I *have* served mankind for thousands of years," Galmadriel's wry smile was an attempt to cover the bitterness she felt at being rejected from her home, "and look where it has gotten me."

Lips twitching and head tilted, Pam assessed Galmadriel who clasped her hands tightly together to stop them from trembling. "I still don't think you've told us your name."

"Galmadriel."

Before she could stop herself, Pam asked, "Your parents lose a bet with the naming fairies?"

Where does she think I'm from? Galmadriel thought indignantly, *Neverland?* "There are no fairies in..." It took a moment for the sarcasm to register, "Funny."

"You got a nickname? Something a little less..." Pam flapped a hand and Galmadriel thought she was trying hard not to say the word 'weird'.

Nickname? It took a few seconds for Galmadriel's mind to supply the concept before racing through several possibilities. Gallie...Gaddie? Ugh, no. Madriel. Worse. Addie...Maddie? No. No. No.

"Adriel. You can call me Adriel." If she was going to be stuck with a new human life, she might as well have a new name to go along with it. Yes, Adriel would do nicely, and she made a mental note to think of herself that way from now on.

Years behind a counter selling pastries had turned Pam into a shrewd judge of character. One who knew Adriel had chosen her new name right on the spot. For her part, Adriel did her best to look like someone intrinsically honest and capable who was reeling from some recent calamity. Because that is exactly who she was. You know—minus the huge secret about her past. Oh, and the possibility of following in the footsteps of other fallen angels and turning evil.

"So which is it? Man, family, or the law?"

"Pardon?" Adriel wrinkled her forehead in confusion.

Pam sighed "I can see you're in trouble, probably on the run, and if I take you on, I need to know what kind of trouble and how long before it comes knocking on my door."

"I am quite alone in this world and have broken no laws here. You will not have any trouble from me." Her words were nothing more than the truth. Adriel met Pam's questioning gaze with a level look, then waited for judgment. As close as she tried to keep her emotions, Pam's face betrayed them. She wanted to believe—Adriel could see that—but there was still a hint of skepticism.

Pam took her time answering.

"Fine, I'll give you a shot. I just need you to fill out some employment forms."

Employment forms. Adriel rummaged around in her memory for the meaning. When she found it, her stomach dropped. "Employment forms?" She repeated in order to buy some time to figure out how she would deal with her lack of verifiable identity. Nothing came to mind as Hamlin skillfully maneuvered the converted delivery van down a narrow alley running behind a series of connected buildings. He parked the truck, shot Adriel an encouraging look over his shoulder, and disappeared through a gray door.

"Come inside," Threading her way past wheeled racks, Pam detoured into her cluttered office to retrieve a thin folder from a full to bulging file cabinet. Calling out a greeting to someone named Wiletta, Pam gestured for Ariel to take a seat at a tile-topped bistro table positioned near the pastry case.

The first thing that hit Adriel was the sweet aromas of sugar and yeast. Her gut churned out a response. Whatever went with that intoxicating scent, she wanted to wrap herself up in it and wallow.

Pam slapped the folder down on the mottled-blue Formica and took a seat. "I'll need to ask you a few questions about...." Then she noticed Adriel, arms folded across her middle to ease the aching emptiness, eying the case with a lascivious stare.

"Have you eaten today?" Pam's curiosity increased by the minute.

"No," Adriel admitted while the gnawing feeling grew more intense, and a strange growling noise erupted from her belly. She looked down in consternation before turning her flaming face away from Pam's amused stare.

Bustling back behind the counter, Pam pulled a loaf of crusty bread from some hidden area, cut a generous slice, and slathered it with butter. A handful of grapes and some slices of cheese joined the plated bread on a small tray, which she carried back to the table after adding two coffee mugs and a pot of decaf.

Pushing the plate across, she poured two cups from the steaming pot. Though it was not the first time Adriel had smelled the enticing aroma of brewed coffee, it was the first time she had ever connected the sense of scent to hunger—or to a desire to gulp down copious amounts of the dark brew.

She hesitated even though the food called to her like a siren to a sailor.

"My pockets are empty."

Pam merely pointed to the plate and barked out a command, "Eat." Fierce of face, she expected compliance.

After the first tentative bite, Adriel closed her eyes to better savor her initial experience with the sense of taste. This was simple fare and yet, the lightly salted butter melted on her tongue to perfectly compliment the textures of the aromatic bread—chewy, crisp crust around a pillowy, moist interior. Next, she sampled a bit of the cheese and found it pungent with complex layers of sharpness. When the first grape burst sweetly between her teeth, she nearly cried from the basic

17

pleasure of eating the tart fruit. Her concentration narrowed to this single act, and she quickly demolished the contents of the plate.

"Feel better?" Pam asked with a raised eyebrow and an indulgent twinkle in her eye, after watching her prospective new employee mop up the last remaining bread crumbs with a fingertip and pop them into her mouth.

"Yes, thank you." The words seemed inadequate. Food was one aspect of being human Adriel could grow to like.

Sliding the plate out of the way, Pam opened the folder to pull out a sheaf of papers. She flipped them over and slid them across the table, along with a pen pulled from an apron pocket, before excusing herself to help Hamlin finish restocking the mobile bakery.

Though she busied herself for the next ten minutes, Pam's gaze weighed heavy on Adriel every time she passed by. She kept one eye on the folder while simultaneously appraising a tray of maple glazed donuts studded with bits of bacon Wiletta slid into a spotlessly polished glass case.

A good ten minutes passed before Adriel pulled the folder open to leaf through its contents, reading each sheet of paper carefully before returning it to the pile. Finding gainful employment was going to be a lot harder than she thought.

"Something wrong?" Pam ignored Hamlin, who was making exaggerated gestures toward his watch in an attempt to hurry things along.

"I'm sorry. I can't do this." Adriel flipped the folder closed with a final pat.

"It's a standard W-2 and an employment history. What parts are giving you trouble?"

"All of it. I can't give you my former address, or any of the forms of identification on the list, and my employment history only includes a very long but unpaid position."

"So you *are* in trouble."

"Not exactly." A dull throb pulsed painfully in Adriel's temple. What could she say that would sound plausible? She didn't want to prevaricate but who would believe the entire truth? Saying "I am an angel who fell out of heaven and I forgot to bring my wallet" was more likely to land her in trouble than get her a job. Not least because she had never owned a wallet in the first place.

"This is my first day as a...here." *Could I sound more stupid?* Adriel wondered. She stood to leave, "I've been turned out from my home, and now I am adrift in the world with nothing but the clothes on my back. Your sign said you need help, and I can help, but not if I have to fill out the forms or answer questions about my past. Tell me what I can do to repay you for the food before I leave." The words came out of her in a rush. It was the best she had to offer and it was a total failure. *She* was a total failure.

For a moment there was silence as Pam flashed her best pointed stare, presumably to search for evidence of a lie. Chin up with just a hint of pride, Adriel stood firm under the scrutiny. Her words were the simple truth, or as much of it as she felt safe to provide. She turned toward the door.

"No, stay. I'm not sending you out to live in the street." Not when you clearly wouldn't last a day. That last bit Pam kept to herself, but no special powers were needed to read between those lines. "I have an idea if you're willing to work for room and board."

"Thank you." Grateful tears stung Adriel's eyes for a second before she blinked them back. "Room and board? What kind of board? Like oak or cherry?"

Pam rolled her eyes. "Look, I own a small cabin about half a mile from here. It needs work and a good cleaning, but you can stay there rent free in return for a bit of DIY."

"DIY?"

"Do It Yourself—fixing up the place. It's not much but it has the basic amenities and the roof doesn't leak, so you'll be warm and dry."

"Is that where the board comes in? You want me to use it to fix up the cabin?" Okay, so a millennium around humans had not provided Adriel with every concept.

Pam grinned, "Room and board means I'll supply your meals in return for the work on the cabin—where you will stay." She tilted her head, "You'll need a little spending money, too. If you can work a cash register and handle a tray, you can take the lunch crowd a couple days a week—as long as you don't mind working for tips. We serve soup and sandwiches from 11 am to 2 pm every day. You can fill in on the days we do an afternoon run in the truck."

"Tips?"

"When you provide good service, people pay extra money like a reward. Where did you say you came from again?"

This topic needed to be put to rest. "Somewhere far away from here where it seems I am no longer welcome." Pam reached across the table to give Adriel's hand a pat. Sympathy flowed through the touch of her skin, "You'll tell me about it when you're ready, but for now, I don't need to know."

With the decision made, Pam pushed away from the table and got back to business.

"Hamlin, go on ahead with the truck. I'll get Adriel settled and meet you in Saint's Square." She hustled Adriel out the door and into a Jeep parked a few spaces away..

The moment the door shut behind her passenger, Pam stabbed the gas. The Jeep shot down the street like a rocket. A little over half a mile later, she tromped on the brake with equal force and whipped into a short, rutted driveway where Adriel got the first glimpse of her new home. Cabin had been a kind word for the building. Shack would have been more appropriate. Honestly, hovel wasn't far off the mark.

What little paint had once coated the weathered exterior had deteriorated to no more than peeled shavings still in the process of being whisked from the surface by the wind. A pair of non-matching windows flanked the door, one painted red and the other blue. Still, the roof line was straight, and the porch floor felt solid and true.

Turning the key in the lock, Pam shot a sympathetic look over her shoulder and cautioned, "The last person to live here was a pack rat. Just be warned." The door swung open. With trepidation Adriel followed her new landlord inside.

Talking quickly now, Pam pointed out the few positive features of the tiny cabin. "The range and refrigerator are newish, and there's one of those stackable washer/dryer combos in the bathroom. There are clean sheets and blankets in the chest at the foot of the bed."

"Bed?"

"Through that door." Pam gestured toward the opposite end of the cabin, but all there was to see was box after box piled to the ceiling, leaving only a maze-like path between them.

"Door?" Adriel repeated blankly.

"It's there behind the wall of boxes. A little cleaning could make this into a cute place."

"A little cleaning?" Adriel felt like a parrot stuck on repeat. Pam deserved a prize for understatement of the year—maybe for the century. "What do the boxes contain?"

"Probably a bunch of junk. My uncle lived here until…early onset dementia set in a few years ago; I had to put him into a nursing home this spring and since he had no kids of his own, all of this," she waved a hand expansively, "turned into my problem. There's been no time to even think about sorting it all out."

"Sisyphus would have chosen his rock compared to this task," Adriel muttered.

"Who?" Pam's brow wrinkled. "Did everyone have a weird name where you come from? I'll bet you grew up in a commune. That would explain a lot."

"Sisyphus? Mythological figure sentenced to push a large boulder up the same hill every day for eternity, and no, I did not grow up." Catching the raised eyebrow Pam shot her, Adriel quickly added, "in a commune."

Pam threaded her way through the piles of detritus to the one space in the cabin that was relatively clear: the kitchenette. Mismatched lower cabinets sprawled from the refrigerator in one corner to the stove in the other, with the

21

sink halfway between. The upper cabinets were all the same except for the handles. Adriel watched impassively while Pam reached down behind the small range and presumably switched on the gas. Once each burner had been tested, she moved on to plug in the fridge.

"Let me just get the water turned on and fire up the water heater." She grabbed a couple of tools from a drawer near the sink, then bit her lip as she looked around critically. "I'll stop by Bud's Shop Rite on my way home and pick up a few essential items. This mess is worse than I remembered. Sorting through the boxes alone will be enough to earn you a year's worth of rent. I'll stock up the fridge." She pulled open a few cabinets to see of there might be any usable foodstuffs left in them.

Her eyes met Adriel's, chagrin on her face when she found nothing more than a dozen cans of something called SPAM. "And the cabinets. And some cleaning supplies. And I'll have the phone line reconnected." Twisting her body to reach under the sink, Pam did whatever it was she needed to do. Adriel couldn't tell, other than that it involved some banging and a fair amount of cussing.

Satisfied, finally, Pam brushed a bit of dust from her hair and turned on the tap. Whooshing noises preceded sporadic gushes of water before the flow settled into a solid stream. Adriel watched Pam duck behind a stand of boxes. From what Adriel assumed was the bathroom came a series of similar noises followed by a faint, "All set."

"I'll be back later," Pam called over her shoulder as she breezed out the door leaving Adriel to look around her new home. As an angel, being thankful was eternally ingrained into her the very molecules of her being; however, today she was no longer an angel, and neither was she thankful. Disgusted, annoyed, and abandoned were closer to the description.

All she wanted was to go to the one place where it seemed she was no longer welcome: home.

***

In the silence that fell after Pam closed the door behind her, Adriel felt more alone than ever before. Despair settled deep in her chest, stole her breath in a suffocating blanket of sadness. A ringing noise sounded in her ears that had nothing to do with bells or phones. Stumbling to the table, she sat and dropped her head onto folded arms while the stinging in her eyes turned to a flood of burning tears. Being cut off from everything she had ever known—her work, her identity as an angel—and landed here, amid a shallow layer of dust and some poor soul's castoffs felt like more punishment than she deserved. What was she supposed to do now?

Sinking lower into self-pity, the blackness descended until she cursed herself for the stupid choices that had led her to this place; to this time; to this body. This treacherous body with its hunger and pain and tears; she hated it more than she hated pure evil. And she still had to pee.

Too busy wallowing in misery, she missed the rustling sound of the pet door when it opened, the padding of tiny feet as the cat approached. When a tentative paw batted at her hair, Adriel shot out of the chair with her heart hammering in a chest that, before today, had never known the base nature of fear. Today, it had known little else.

Gifted with the ability to become corporeal when necessary, while an angel, her body had always been a thing made of energy, not mass. She was unaccustomed to the way emotions affected the physical.

"Was that really necessary? You scared me," she wagged a finger at the black cat, who merely regarded her with an unblinking green stare. If he could have, he probably would have smirked at her. Calmer now, she decided a little company might make life here more bearable. A loud yawl split the air.

"Howling at me is not polite."

As though he understood the words, the cat gracefully turned to spill languidly to the floor. A short span of living in the wild must have honed his hunting skills, since he appeared stout and healthy, but based on his actions, he preferred a dinner he didn't have to chase down and kill. To emphasize his point, he sat back on well-toned haunches and loosed a second plaintive yawl before stalking purposefully toward one particular low cabinet. A delicate paw reached out to brush against the white enamel, nails making a noise that set Adriel's teeth on edge. She would have done anything to stop the cringe-worthy feeling of her skin crawling, so she opened the cabinet to find an unopened bag of kibble and several small round cans stacked alongside.

Seeing the human had finally gotten the hint, the feline pranced his way across the floor toward a pair of bowls. One was labeled food, the other, water. Well, that was clear enough. Adriel shook bits of kibble from the bag and filled the water dish.

Another disdainful look from the cat had her choosing one of the cans and taking a closer look to see how it opened. A firm pull on the ring did the trick. The strong smell of tuna filling the air made her nose wrinkle.

She dumped half the can's smelly contents on top of the kibble—which wasn't easy with the cat trying to shove his head into the bowl the entire time—then stepped back to watch him eat with gusto. The sound of contented purring went a long way toward soothing Adriel's rough-edged nerves, and brought the ghost of a smile to her face.

As soon as he finished bolting his meal, the cat issued a small belch and leapt back to the table, then up onto the nearest pile of boxes He circled twice, sprawled on his back, and, still purring quietly, fell promptly asleep.

Cheered a little by the cat's presence, curiosity and urgent need sent Adriel wandering through the maze of boxes. Despite the sheer volume of things crammed into the tiny cabin, Pam's uncle had been somewhat tidy in his personal habits. Under a fine layer of dust that had accumulated in his absence, the bathroom fixtures were surprisingly clean. This room had stayed relatively uncluttered—probably because there hadn't been room for more than his personal toiletries. Those, thankfully, had gone along with him to his new home, leaving the shelves empty of everything except a stack of linens. The topmost facecloth Adriel sacrificed to rag status, and used it to wipe away every tiny mote of dust.

Looking at her reflection in the beveled glass hanging above old porcelain, she saw the face she had ended up with. This, at least, was one of her favorites. A fall of auburn hair, a sprinkling of freckles dotting creamy smooth skin, and lips the color of good red wine. Eyes the blue of a winter cloud, rimmed with red from crying gazed back at her from smudged hollows. She reached out one hand toward the mirror, the other touching her chin just to make sure the vision before her was real. A pinch just below the apple of her cheek pulled up a stain of angry red. And it hurt. Yes. Totally real.

She did what she had come in here to do. This human body's plumbing require a lot more maintenance than she expected. Next, Adriel decided to explore the bedroom hiding somewhere behind the wall of boxes. A circuitous path skirted the stacks blocking the way between the bathroom and bedroom. Out of necessity, clearing that route would become her first priority. The physical labor should help take her mind off other things.

Moving the first stack of bins and boxes out onto the porch—the only other place where they would fit—took longer than expected when she discovered the only way to navigate the maze was to lift each box over her head.

"I didn't sign on for this." All the activity had wakened the cat who blinked back at her. "Well, I didn't." Adriel flexed sore muscles.

The sound of footsteps on the porch warned of Pam's knock. Adriel opened the door to find her new landlord burdened with plastic sacks. Cleaning supplies and food disappeared into cabinets and the fridge with Pam's usual efficiency.

"You've been busy," she nodded her approval. "Okay, walk down to the shop in the morning and we'll get started on your training. The phone should be on; here's my number." Pam jotted something on a small pad. "Call if you need anything."

"I'll be fine," Adriel wasn't convinced, but wanted to put a good face on things. "Oh, what's the cat's name?"

"Winston's back? I've been trying to catch him for weeks. I was afraid he'd gone feral."

Adriel gestured to where the black body once again sprawled atop a pile of boxes. "He seems quite tame to me. The name suits him."

"Uncle Craig will be pleased." A shadow of strong emotion crossed Pam's face and then was gone. "Anyway, I'll get out of your way—you look like you could do with some sleep. See you in the morning."

Sleep sounded like a great plan, but Adriel's stomach had other ideas. Thoughtfully, Pam had included a couple pre-made sandwiches in the items now filling the refrigerator. Stomach blissfully full, Adriel made her way to the bedroom.

A tubular metal headboard arched over a twin bed bared to the striped mattress. A single bulb with a pull chain threaded through a plastic clip-on shade illuminated the room. From the end of the chain switch, a length of heavy string traced a path to the headboard, where it was tied around the top of the frame. Pam's uncle liked his conveniences. Once in bed, he could pull the string to turn off the light without having to fumble in the dark. Right where Pam had said they would be, pillows, sheets, and blankets rested, neatly folded, in a hand hewn wooden box at the foot of the bed. Bright patterns worked into the soft bed coverings would loan some warmth to the otherwise austere room. When she opened the single window, sunflower-patterned curtains fluttered in the cool night breeze.

Picking through the contents of the chest, Adriel chose a pair of nearly matching floral sheets. Getting them spread onto the bed turned out to be a chore when the cat, hearing the first snap of sheets being flipped, decided a game of 'romp the bed' was in order. Paws splayed out for balance and eyes bulging, he leaped and pounced to hinder Adriel's every effort until she couldn't help laughing at his antics.

"Go on you crazy beastie."

Chapter Two

An unfamiliar feeling crept along Adriel's shoulders until it settled into her neck and winched the muscles into a taut mass of pulsing fiber. Sometime after midnight, Adriel nudged the cat aside, and collapsed onto the narrow bed to let the soft purring lull her toward sleep. Fatigue lay over her like a blanket. How did these frail humans ever manage to build cities, when just moving a dozen or so boxes from one place to another could cause such an ache?

At least the path between bedroom and bathroom was clear.

When a little furry head nudged against her hand, she absently stroked the softness and slipped into deep slumber. It felt as though only minutes had passed when she was startled awake by a noise so insidiously annoying Adriel could not believe her ears.

Boop, boop, boop.

"Oh, what is that?" She asked the cat, who declined to answer.

The noise increased. A series of crashing and banging sounds punctuated the cacophony of whistling beeps cutting through her brain like a knife. Slapping hands over her ears, Adriel stumbled to the window and peered out to see a group of large vehicles lining the road.

Painted a deceivingly cheerful yellow, the fleet of machines worked busily. Oddly shaped trucks inched along behind a machine that moved forward using a type of oval track where the wheels should have been. A mechanical arm tipped by a clawed bucket reached down to scoop a great load of dirt and rocks from the shallow ditch running alongside the road. Without rhyme or reason, the load of dirt and rocks was then dumped out a short distance away. What was the point of moving scoops of earth only to dump them a few feet away?

Humans certainly found some odd ways to occupy their time.

With the chance of falling asleep amid the racket nothing more than a distant wish, Adriel poured a generous amount of kibble into a bowl for the cat, and made her way to the bathroom to take stock of her appearance.

Wrinkled clothes looking like they'd been slept in—because they had—hair a mussed up tangle, and pillow creases lined her face: not pretty. She quirked an eyebrow at her reflection, and did the best she could to right the damage to her hair. The clothes were another thing entirely. In her angelic past, taking on human form came complete with the appropriate outfit as part of the energy signature. There wasn't time right now to mourn the loss of that ability. She had to attend a training session with Pam today.

Not feeling her absolute best, Adriel began the short walk to the bakery, where she hoped for some blessed quiet.

Even the dinging of the little bell on the door jangled against sleep-deprived nerves, and for whatever reason, the sight of Pam's cheerful face flared annoyance like a match to a flame.

"You're early." Pam raised an eyebrow at Adriel's scowling face and hunched over posture. "Not a morning person?"

"Apparently not. Noise. So much noise." Adriel lifted a hand to rub at eyes gritty from lack of sleep.

"You can thank your neighbor for that. Lydia Keough decided the ditches in front of her house needed work. Never mind that all the runoff travels on the other side of the road. Waste of taxpayer's money, digging ditches for no reason."

During her diatribe, Pam had been busy breaking eggs into a pan on top of a six-burner commercial-grade stove. She snagged a couple slices of bacon from the pile waiting to be candied, crumbled them into a topping for maple glazed donuts, and added those to the plates before gesturing for Adriel to join her.

The food smelled wonderful until Pam upended a bottle of ketchup onto her eggs and the sharp, tangy odor of the condiment assailed Adriel's nose. She shook her head with a grimace when Pam offered the container, then scooped a small portion of the fluffy eggs onto her fork to take a tentative bite.

Pam watched with eyes full of questions. From what she could tell, this was Adriel's first time eating scrambled eggs. How could that be? The woman was in her thirties, at least. Had she been locked in a basement somewhere for all that time? There was a story, and Pam wanted to hear it.

Instead, she made small talk while she plied her newest employee with food and then offered "Coffee?"

Ah, stimulants.

"Please." The taste was off-putting, but if it burned away the fog in Adriel's brain, she could deal with it. The first sip scalded her tongue, which was probably not the worst thing since it deadened the taste buds to the bitterness. She took another.

Grinning at the distaste on Adriel's face, Pam poured a dollop of cream to lighten the brew. Better, but still too strong. Without being asked, she stirred in a spoonful of sugar.

Now that was more like it. The sweetness teased a more pleasing flavor from the steaming liquid, and Adriel began to enjoy the flavor of the drink almost as much as the way it cleared her head.

"Come on back," Pam called over her shoulder, her step jaunty. How did the woman manage to be that energetic this early in the morning? Moving quickly, Pam selected items from around the office: an apron, a hat with Just Desserts emblazoned across the front, and a name tag joined the pile on the small desk while she provided a running commentary on the inner workings of the bakery.

Centuries of watching humans, Adriel was beginning to realize, did not nearly give one enough experience to understand the intricacies of their lives.

She had watched civilizations rise and fall for reasons she found completely frivolous. She had watched over kings and paupers. Now, her biggest concern was remembering how many donuts were in a baker's dozen. What choice did she have? She followed Pam into the kitchen, where the sweet smell of sugar combined with the yeasty scent of freshly baking bread into a heavenly aroma.

Hearing voices coming toward him, Hamlin Paine turned around with a welcoming smile. Without thinking, he let loose a low whistle that carried his thoughts to Adriel, who stopped walking in surprise when she heard them clearly.

Hot. And that hair. I'd like to bury my hands in it to see if the strands are as alive as they look. Porcelain skin, eyes of burning blue, and tall enough to nearly look me in the eye.

Not that Adriel did. Face flaming in embarrassment, she turned away to hide jumbled emotions. It must have been a fluke—a random pulse of residual angel ability. It probably wouldn't happen again. Best to put all thoughts of the past behind her and adjust to this new life. Adriel concentrated on observing the room around her.

Compact but well fitted out, the kitchen had been designed with economy of effort and efficiency in mind. Dry ingredients lined shelves on the right hand side of the mixing station; containers and utensils were stored above and beneath the stainless steel surface. The baker needed only to turn around to pull wet ingredients from the double coolers.

At the other end of the space, enormous commercial ovens took up the end wall, while a six burner cook top backed the short wall overlooking the sales area of the bakery. Golden-brown bits of dough bobbed and bubbled in the commercial frying station—their scent whispered of sugary sin.

As she watched, a rack rose from the oily depths to convey the puffs of cooked dough to a draining tray.

Talking rapidly, Hamlin explained how Pam had given him carte blanch to design the space so that the work followed a natural progression. A narrow doorway between a large metal cabinet he called a proofer and a section of counter dominated by two commercial mixers led to another room containing an industrial type dishwasher and a deep, triple sink.

Everything was scrupulously clean. Everything except for Hamlin himself. Dabs of icing clung to his apron, and most of his lanky, six-foot-five frame looked like it had been dipped in a vat of dry ingredients. Both hands were covered in the sticky, sweet substance he had just turned out onto a floured board.

Still talking and with no regard for his unkempt state, he reached a hand toward Adriel. What did he want? Then she remembered humans touched hands as a form of greeting. She was just about to make contact when he yanked his hand back. Now, what?. Had she hesitated too long? Hurt his feelings?

"Er, sorry," Hamlin returned to his kneading. "Sticky fingers are a hazard around here." Cheerful eyes sparkled while he worked steadily at developing gluten, and the dough slowly turned elastic.

"So I see."

"Hamlin's a genius with pastry, and so is Wiletta—you'll meet her next time. They went to culinary school together." Pam skirted the table to grab a tray containing two dozen cinnamon rolls, which she quickly and expertly glazed with a sticky, white coating. Despite the eggs Adriel had just eaten, her mouth watered.

She could get to like this eating thing.

***

The sun was just starting to burn through the thinner places of a low-lying fog shadowing parts of the town of Longbrook under a cool, damp shroud. A million sparkling mirrored drops turned every sunlight-touched surface into a fairyland that faded back to normal in a matter of minutes as the heated sunshine drank away the moisture.

For the second day in a row, Adriel shot awake when the incessant whistle of heavy equipment reversing outside the cabin penetrated her dreams. Closer to her bedroom window today, the noises were louder than ever.

Rubbing sleep from her eyes, she gave in to the temptation to utter a word forbidden to angels. "Shasta daisy." Nope, not even close to what she had intended to say. Why was the naughty filter still in place if she wasn't an angel anymore?

Denied the release to be found in yelling obscenities, she clutched the pillow to her head in a desperate attempt to block out the racket. Another hour. That's all she needed, just one more hour of sleep. Okay, maybe two.

When the noise cut off abruptly, Adriel sighed with relief before relaxing back into a light slumber that only lasted until the unmistakable sound of an argument forced her fully awake again.

She threw off the covers and stomped over to the window to twitch aside the curtain. Even with her excellent hearing, the glass muted enough of the sound that she couldn't make out what they were saying. One little nudge on the sash let in the raised voices and heated words flying thick and fast between two people standing at the edge of the trench. Adriel never got a clear look at the woman with the sharp voice, but the burly man dressed in blue jeans, a white tee, and a yellow hard hat pulled low on his forehead seemed to be in charge of the work.

"It's not deep enough," insisted the woman.

"Don't tell me how to do my job. You may have persuaded the town to sign off on this ridiculous waste of time and money, but that doesn't make you a construction engineer. This is plenty deep enough for a ditch that will never get any use."

She ignored this piece of truth. "Fine, then at least line it with stones so the grass won't grow back."

"Get back inside and let me handle the heavy lifting; or do you think your big mouth qualifies you to run a loader, too?"

"I don't care for your tone."

"And I don't care for your meddling. I didn't ask for this job, and getting stuck with it cost me a lucrative contract. Look around, do my guys seem happy to be here? Holding the winter road maintenance contract over my head if I didn't drop everything for this is nothing more than blackmail. Go home, Lydia. Before I give in to the temptation to toss you in that hole."

All Adriel could see of the woman was a fleeting profile: a petite, tight-postured body, chin length hair, and a longish nose firmly pointed up as she retreated into the rapidly dissolving mist. There was something eerie about the way the sun fell through the thinning shroud to illuminate her body.

Just as Adriel made ready to turn away, the sun glinted off of a shiny object across the way. A gully etched by time and water already lined the far side of the narrow road. Beyond the natural ditch, a moss-covered rock wall bordered several acres of mature evergreen trees.

Another flare of sun off metal helped Adriel pinpoint the exact spot where a bicycle leaned up against the trunk of a massive pine with branches spaced for easy climbing. Following the trunk upward with her eyes, she caught the motion when one branch rustled a bit harder than the wind would allow. Adriel had to squint to see the boy who perched there, watching the workers with a happy grin on his face.

The charming sight wasn't enough, though, to improve her mood. Adriel slammed the pane down in disgust, and stomped into the kitchen to measure ground coffee and water into the odd-looking appliance on the counter. She thought she had watched Pam closely enough to know what to do. Put the funny paper filter into the basket, add eight scoops of grounds, and pour a potful of water into the reservoir.

It didn't make sense to make a full pot of the brew for just one person, so she filled the coffeemaker only halfway before placing the carafe in its cradle and punching the button. In her opinion, the beverage really was an acquired taste. It smelled wonderful, and always provided a burst of energy, so the benefits outweighed the slightly bitter flavor.

Funny, this potful looked different from the coffee at the bakery. Even with a generous dollop of creamer, it only lightened slightly. Adriel added a little sweetener, stirred, and took a sip. When the dark tang of it hit her tongue like a sledgehammer, she raced to spit it into the sink. UGH, what happened? If looks could scorch plastic and metal, the coffeemaker would have been nothing but a smoking ruin spread over the kitchen counter.

Snatching up the bag of grounds, she read the directions and quickly learned her mistake. Less water means less coffee. Simple logic.

The second attempt looked, smelled, and tasted more palatable as she cradled the mug in both hands. She wasn't scheduled to work for several more hours yet, and with nothing else to do, she fed Winston before looking around at the mess still left to wade through. Clearing one small area hardly made a dent in the project.

At this rate, she would still be unpacking and sorting whatever was in all these boxes come snowfall.

That thought spurred her to choose a stack and get to work. With the bedroom doorway cleared, the next logical step was to make some space in the tiny seating area. According to Pam, there was a sofa somewhere behind the labyrinthine wall of bins and boxes. Common sense told her to work from the front to the back, which meant starting with the top two from the stack of plastic bins blocking access to the area.

The first, she discovered once she'd pried off the lid, was cram-packed with brightly-colored labels Craig had peeled from cans of vegetables. The next box contained empty tin cans of various sizes, presumably the ones formerly sporting all of those labels. Once stomped flat, the cans went into the recycling bin along with the similar contents of a third tote. The labels went into a bag to be recycled separately.

The bottom box from the pile, thankfully, contained something more interesting than trash. Books. About thirty or so, and all of the same type: cookbooks. All Adriel had time for was a quick glance through some of the pages, but the way the glossy pictures made her mouth water had her setting these aside for further perusal. The one with the melted cheese dip called fondue looked especially interesting.

Of all the inconveniences that came with a mortal body, eating was the only one she enjoyed.

Showers, though? Those seemed to require a set of skills she might never master. The water was either too cold or too hot and shampoo kept getting in her eye. Who had thought it was a good idea to make things slippery when wet? Twice the plastic bottle had squirted out of her hands to thump heavily into the tub—both times glancing painfully off one of her feet. The suds took forever to rinse out of her hair. A tedious process at best.

Getting dressed, at least, was quick. She only owned the one set of clothes which, thanks to the little washer and dryer, were now clean and unwrinkled. A half dozen tee shirts found in the bottom of the blanket box were now piled in the top dresser drawer. Two sizes too large, Adriel had decided to turn them into sleepwear.

So many new things to worry about.

Chapter Three

How hard could it be to patch up a few broken shingles? Adriel had tools, nails, shingles, and a book with pictures explaining the process. Piece of cake. Why did people say that? What does cake have to do with anything? Fitting in with mortals meant having to embrace a lot of strange language. Maybe another book would provide the answer to the cake question. Craig's shelves held an eclectic mix of tomes; she'd have to look through them to see.

Selecting the right sized shingle was easy enough, but juggling it with the hammer and nail proved infinitely more difficult. Before she could bring the tool to bear, the nail slipped out of her fingers to land on the porch floor and roll, inevitably, between the cracks to the dirt below. The third time it happened, she muttered an expletive.

"Flink." Angel filter struck again.

"The trick is to start the nail before you set the shingle into place."

Frowning, Adriel whirled to see a strange man standing at the edge of the porch. Her startled green eyes locked onto a pair the blue-gray of storm clouds on a winter day. His twinkled while hers fired.

"Who are you?" The hammering of her heart came from being startled, of that she was certain. Mostly.

"Callum McCord. We're neighbors." Elbows resting on the top of her porch railing, Callum seemed in no hurry to move along.

"Oh. I see." The newly human part of Adriel insisted on cataloging his physical attributes. Those soft gray eyes under a canopy of heavy, dark lashes winked out at her from a face that could have been chiseled on a statue back home. Wet hair slicked back from his face appeared jet black, but would probably dry to mahogany. A pair of cheerful dimples flashed into place every time he smiled.

Before she could lock it down, her gaze lowered to take in the rest of him.

Broad, tanned-to-perfection shoulders bared to the sun by some type of sleeveless outer garment rested above a chest that stretched that garment tightly. Made from orange-colored ribbed material that looked soft to the touch, it skimmed down the taut plain of his belly to where it was tucked into a pair of well-worn jeans.

While the mortal inside her enjoyed the spectacle, Adriel's inner angel insisted his soul was the more important component, and she should stop admiring his form.

"Adriel." She held out her hand in the human form of greeting, then bit her lip gently when the clasp of his sent a frisson of energy through her that any normal woman would have recognized as attraction. She found it unsettling.

"Want me to show you?"

His words seemed out of place now that her mind had wandered away from the earlier conversation. "What?"

"The shingle. Starting the nail." His tone, one that indicated he was beginning to wonder if Adriel was scatterbrained, was punctuated by a single raised eyebrow.

"Oh." She handed him the hammer. "Go right ahead." *Shake it off*, she told herself.

Callum picked a shingle from the top of the bundle. "So you lay the shingle down flat like this," he bent to lay the thin piece of wood on the porch floor, "take a nail," he held one up to show her, "position it where it should go, and gently tap it once or twice. Just enough to start the nail into the wood, but not hard enough to push it all the way through." With a deft motion he applied just the right amount of force. When he lifted the shingle up from the floor, the nail held its place.

Then, going to the wall, he slid the shingle into position and tapped the nail with two harder strikes to drive it home.

"See? Simple."

Still a bit flustered over the rush of unwanted feelings, Adriel reached for the polite words the situation warranted. "Yes, thank you." What she really wanted to say was, given enough time, she would have come up with the idea on her own. It might even have been true. But probably not. Who knew what would have come out of her if she'd tried to voice the lie.

"What do you think of Mrs. Keough's ditch." The brightly colored plastic chair creaked under his weight as Callum made himself at home on the porch. The way he kicked his feet out in front of him made it look like he planned on staying for a long visit.

"I could have lived without the incessant beeping in the morning."

"Not a morning person?"

"Why does everyone keep asking me that? Do I have a sign pinned on my back?"

"Turn around and let me look." Callum's tone shivered over newly discovered nerves.

To cover her discomfort, Adriel turned away to select her next shingle. Having watched him, she now knew exactly what to do. Two gentle taps set the nail as expertly as Callum's had done. If she hadn't already had it, her sure movements would have gotten his full attention. One eyebrow quirked while he watched her set the shingle and drive the nail home.

"You're a quick study."

"What? It's not rocket science. Now, what were we talking about?"

"The ditch. What do you think of Lydia's masterpiece? It's the big topic around town. That and where did the gorgeous creature slinging pie and cake over at Just Desserts come from." Face flaming, Adriel searched her mind for a diplomatic answer.

"Surely my opinion on town matters is unimportant."

"And you're not going to settle my curiosity on the other question, either. Don't worry, I already know where you came from." Callum's booted feet hit the floor with a heavy sound as he levered himself out of the flimsy plastic chair.

"Oh really?"

"Sure." Callum swept a look from Adriel's head to her toes, "Woman as fine as you must have come from heaven."

How could he know? Adriel's pulse pounded until her ears drummed the sound. *It was just a lucky guess. Nothing more.*

"See you later, Angel." Callum tossed the words carelessly over one shoulder and walked away without a backward glance, leaving Adriel to sink into the chair still warm from his body heat.

***

"That was one fine looking man." Adriel twisted around so fast the legs on the chair couldn't keep up with her. The whole thing started to go over, and if her reflexes were any less keen, Adriel would have gone down with it. Instead, she regained her footing and squared off against the newcomer who was now leaning sideways for a better view of Callum walking away.

"Estelle." Appalled at the appreciation on the newly-minted angel's face for a pair of tight jeans molded over a firmly packed behind, Adriel sputtered, "What are you doing here. Stop that." She leaned over to put her body between Estelle and the view. What made it even worse was Estelle appearing in the form Adriel knew best—an eighty-year-old with kind blue eyes surrounded by wrinkles born of laughter. That grandmotherly face ogling a man half the age she'd been when she took her last breath was not just unsettling; it was scandalous. "Gawking at mortals is not allowed."

"Really? No one told me." Estelle shrugged off the faux pas without an iota of repentance.

Since Estelle was in corporeal form, Adriel gave her a nudge. "Come inside and tell me everything that's happened to you since we lost control of the bridge." So many questions formed in Adriel's mind that she knew choosing the most important ones was going to be impossible.

"He was flirting with you." Estelle made no rush toward the door. Her comment sent heat flaring across Adriel's face. *What am I supposed to do with that information?* Adriel wondered. *Angels don't date.*

But then again, she wasn't an angel. She didn't think. Not anymore.

Completely unaffected by Adriel's stare of rebuke, Estelle chuckled before going inside, where she stopped just inside the door. Shock sent her eyebrows skyward and rounded her mouth into an O. Watching Estelle take in the level of clutter—reduced though it was—of her current abode brought a grin to Adriel's face

"The former tenant liked to collect things." She kept her tone mild.

"So I see." Estelle's gaze searched Adriel for signs of distress and fear. In life, Estelle read people nearly as well as any angel. Gaining guardian status boosted the ability up to devastating.

"I'm sorry. These kitchen chairs are all I have available just now. I'm working on clearing the way to the sofa."

Estelle opened her mouth to say something, thought better of it, and closed her mouth again. Her moment of discomfort set Adriel a little more at ease.

"Julius, he's okay? What happened to the two of you after I...after it happened? You didn't get into trouble because of me did you?"

41

"He's fine. We're guardians on a high profile case. Very important."

Relief sagged Adriel's shoulders. For days now, she'd carried the burden of knowing Julius and Estelle might have been called on to pay for her mistakes. Dropping that weight made her feel lighter than she had in days.

"How much trouble am I in?" A second passed. Estelle tried to cover the hesitation, but Adriel was no slouch in the people reading department either. "Just tell me. I can take it," she said.

To her credit, Estelle made no effort at pretense. "Your situation has created quite a stir among the powers that be."

"You should stay away from me." It felt like an epic understatement when Adriel said it. Trepidation dried her mouth making the words falter. What she never expected was the look of surprise on Estelle's face.

"What makes you say that?"

Now it was Adriel's turn for wide-eyed shock. She gestured toward the room, "I'm a fallen angel, an abomination thrown out of my home to live here among the castoffs of an.." What would be the nicest word to use here? "Eccentric man. I've become human. The only thing I don't understand is how I ended up here instead of in the dark realm." Unexpected bitterness colored her tone, so much for having accepted her situation. "And why did it take three months?"

"Didn't..." Eyebrows lifted into Estelle's hairline. "No, you've had no contact with...anyone." Adriel felt like a bug on a pin when Estelle circled the table to get up close and personal, looking for something inside her. "There's a block on your powers."

"What powers? I'm just a mortal, right? You know, fallen angel. Cast out of heaven. No wings, no powers, just an unyielding hunk of flesh requiring constant care and attention. Showers, food, bathroom....activities." Revulsion made Adriel cringe.

"I had no idea you were completely in the dark." Instead of sitting back down, Estelle put a kettle on to boil for tea.

"Then why don't you enlighten me?"

Cabinets opened and closed. A cup and saucer appeared at Adriel's elbow while Estelle tried to find the right place to begin. "It's complicated. Nothing like this has ever happened before. You've had some fleeting moments where it seemed like you still had access to your abilities." It wasn't a question, somehow she knew, and Adriel nodded.

"But you still don't know what you are."

"A human who occasionally enjoys some fancy extras?"

The force of Estelle's annoyance felt like a living thing, making Adriel wonder if this was how her charges felt when she subjected them to her own annoyance. Maybe she hadn't been as helpful as she'd always thought.

"That's backwards thinking. You are an angel in a human body and I've been given the unenviable task of being *your* assistant or something. There are some ambiguities in my current job description."

"Assistant? Don't you mean guardian? For you to assist me, I'd have to be doing some kind of work and with my powers gone, I'm next to useless. You've been sent on a fool's errand, Estelle. Go back to your high profile case. Leave me to my misery."

Petulance earned Adriel a look that landed with an almost visceral blow. Estelle's mouth firmed into a straight line. Adriel didn't need to read her mind to know Estelle thought she was acting childish. She wasn't wrong either.

Estelle's power trickled through the air to tiptoe across Adriel's limbs, leaving a line of gooseflesh in its wake. Each strand of hair on her arms lifted, and the skin on the back of her neck began to crawl. For the first time ever, Adriel felt guilty for having treated certain mortals to similar experiences.

"Stop that!" Loud in the otherwise quiet room, Adriel's shout startled Estelle, and the energy dissipated enough to release the tightness in her throat. "Estelle, get hold of yourself." If mild annoyance brought out that much power, she was destined to become one formidable angel. Not that Adriel should be the one to guide her. Whoever had sent Estelle to this place had made a terrible mistake.

"I'm sorry. I had no idea." Light swelled from the angel to reach toward Adriel, then pulled back as though Estelle was afraid her touch might cause pain. "This is why I need you to teach me. You're my high profile case." The *you idiot* at the end was only implied.

"You need to learn from someone at the peak of their powers, not some half shell of a former angel who has fallen from grace."

Estelle slapped hands over her eyes, took a deep breath to compose her features, squared her shoulders, then dropped her hands to pin Adriel with a you're-an-idiot look.

"You did not fall from grace."

How could she say that? Falling for what seemed like an eternity—feeling her body rushing toward the earth like a hammer dropping on an anvil; the wrenching, weightless lurching in her belly; the moment when her wings tore away, and then waking up to the heaviness of mortal flesh pressing against her soul—those were not normal experiences for an angel.

Falling was falling, no matter what Estelle wanted to call it.

Then a new thought hit Adriel. If she hadn't fallen from grace, maybe she'd been thrown. Cast out of heaven. That was even worse.

"Just go, Estelle. What do you expect to learn from me if I'm bound for hell?"

For a flashing second Estelle's energy skyrocketed again to a breath-stealing level. Adriel's eyes burned dry, and then the pressure dropped as quickly as it had begun.

"You silly creature. Will you stop feeling sorry for yourself for just long enough to listen to what I am trying to tell you?"

Once upon a time. Okay, three months or so ago, angel or not, Adriel could have tuned into Estelle's thoughts without leaving any sign she'd been there. Now, she could only judge moods based on facial expressions and posture. Set face, shoulders tight with tension, hands resting on her hips, and body leaning slightly forward—Estelle was angry and frustrated.

"You did not fall. You were not cast out." She emphasized each word. "I'm new to angelhood—if that's even a word—and no one really tells me anything useful because, as I said, I'm new. They're keeping your status hush, but from what I've been able to piece together, they theorize the bridge snapping tossed you backward dimensionally turning you into a physical anchor to this world."

"How is being tossed backward different from being cast out?"

"You're not listening to me at all. Angel. In. A. Human. Body," Estelle punctuated each word by tapping the tabletop with her fingers.

"What does that even mean? I have tiny flashes of power I can't control, and everyone from home acts like I don't exist. Believe me, I've called out to everyone I know." That was the burning question in Adriel's mind. Why, if she really was still some sort of an angel, had she been completely cut off from all contact with home?

"No one has told me how it all works. Honestly, I'm beginning to think it's because they don't have a clue. You still have powers. I can feel them inside you. They're—I'm not sure how to describe it exactly—choked with humanity. Muted by being bound to solid flesh, maybe. Or just by you believing they're limited. You'd be the best judge of that, and you'd better plan on figuring it out soon, because this is only the beginning."

"Beginning of what?" Adriel wasn't even sure she wanted to know.

"Your next set of assignments," Estelle said.

"My next set of assignments?"

"What? You thought the powers were done with you? That they wouldn't find a way to capitalize on your unique situation?"

45

"I…" That was exactly what Adriel had been thinking. "What do they want me to do?"

"I'm trusting that when the time comes, we'll both get the answer to that question. The way you took care of Billy the Earthwalker got their attention. You and the others managed to save Logan once he became a vessel." Estelle's nose wrinkled with distaste. No one who knew the details of how Logan degenerated into someone evil enough to carry an Earthwalker had any sympathy for him.

Estelle continued, "Most times the vessel dies. My sense is they want you to continue with some type of work along those lines."

"I made an absolute hash of things. What would make them think doing it again is a good idea?"

"You know, I gave you credit for being smarter than this, and yet, you persist in thinking you are somehow being punished for what happened to Kat." A flicker of some deeper emotion furrowed Estelle's brow. "I worry they want you to enlist my granddaughter and her friends to help," her voice lowered, "Also, I'm scared Julius and I won't be experienced enough to protect you or them."

Shaking off a shiver of worry, Estelle added, "You're going to be contacted soon about your first assignment. Don't ask me for details because I have none to give. Apparently there's a loop and I'm not in it."

One weight came off Adriel's shoulders while another, newer one took its place. One having nothing to do with the physical burden of flesh she now carried, and everything to do with the way she'd gotten it. If she hadn't been entirely cut off from grace, maybe she could still be useful in some capacity, which was all she ever wanted anyway.

Even though it gave her a renewed sense of purpose, she harbored no illusions about the various ways that wish could come back to bite her in the butt.

Chapter Four

"Go outside. Now. Hurry."

Used to this form of communication, Adriel obeyed the voice in her head without thinking twice. Every mission she had ever performed started out with exactly this sort of directive, so it never occurred to her to question.

On the porch, she paused to orient herself. A tugging sensation in her belly directed her to the left. She leapt off the porch and turned obediently in that direction. With each step the sense of urgency grew like a bubble within her, until Adriel was compelled to break into a slow jog past the ragged end of the trench forming the leading edge of the new ditch, and snaked toward the next house farther up the hill.

Unmanned equipment lined both sides of the narrow road, left there by a crew who all lived close enough to go home for lunch.

"Here." Without that voice in her ear, she might have rushed right past the prone form nestled in the tall grass on the other side of the newly-opened earth, so well was it hidden. As it was, she had to retreat and go around the raw hole in the earth to reach the spot where the body lay.

At a dead run now, Adriel called out, "Are you all right? I'm coming." There was no movement or response, and that worried her more than anything. The only sounds she heard were the buzzing of insects and the sharp caw of a crow flying overhead.

Nearing the prone form, Adriel dropped to her knees. The field grass closed in around her with a shushing noise, and above the earthy smells of soil and plants, she caught the coppery tang of fresh blood. Dread at what she might see filled her as she reached out to move the waving stalks away from the injured person's face

A disordered cap of hair stained with red framed a small, gently-lined face. A pair of over-sized glasses with dark frames knocked askew by her fall rested on the bridge of an upturned nose.

Adriel gently tested the tender spot at the victim's throat, hoping to feel the flutter indicating life still flowed. When she detected a single heartbeat, remnants of her angel instinct took over. Adriel knew exactly how little time left to the injured woman. With divine intervention, there was a possibility, however slim, she could be saved. In the past, if it was within the will of providence, Adriel's healing ability would have been more than sufficient. Now, she could only mourn the loss of that power.

"Try."

Ingrained by an eternity of listening to that small voice, Adriel laid hands alongside the prone woman's face and let her body remember what had once come so naturally. Energy channeled through trembling hands to funnel into the bleeding head wound. At only a portion of her normal strength, Adriel knew it probably wouldn't be enough. The woman's injury was so grave it absorbed every ounce of her healing power and still needed more.

All Adriel could hope was what she had was enough to stabilize the poor victim until help could arrive.

"Ma'am if you can hear me, I'm going to get help. Don't move." Confident she had done everything she could for the moment, Adriel sprinted back to the cabin to call 911. With help on the way, she pulled a blanket from the bed and raced back to tuck it around the injured form. While they waited, Adriel kept up a running commentary that earned no response. She only hoped it eased the woman's mind.

"Stay with me, help is on the way."

It was only a few minutes before the sound of wailing sirens soared across the air, and moments later Adriel abandoned her charge in order to meet the first responders and lead them toward where the injured woman lay in the grass.

When a county cruiser pulled up behind the ambulance and Zack Roman stepped out onto the newly-churned gravel to stride toward her with purpose, Adriel got the second shock of the day. His eyes widened with surprise, then narrowed with some other emotion as Zack recognized her. Later, his look said, there would be some explaining to do.

Leaving him unconscious on the floor, arms clutched around the love of his life—the woman he had crossed the rainbow bridge to save—had not been Adriel's finest moment. The past had now come to roost, and she was afraid no explanation for abandoning him or the rest of the group would satisfy.

"Galmadriel," he greeted her tersely, then turned his attention to the scene before him. "That's Lydia Keough." The name rang a bell in Adriel's memory. Pam had mentioned the woman with some venom, if she recalled correctly.

For the next few minutes, Zack listened while the paramedics discussed Lydia's condition. He asked a question or two, and was answered with technical jargon.

While work continued on her head and neck, Zack's keen eyes took in the position of Lydia's body, and when careful hands turned her to get a better look at the wound on the back of her head, they narrowed. Adriel saw the same thing he did. A bloody rock had been positioned to make it look as though a simple fall was the cause of Lydia's injuries, but he was not fooled. Zack was good at his job and could spot a staged scene when he saw one.

Using his cell phone camera, he snapped several shots of Lydia and the rock before pinning Adriel with a look and ordering her in a low voice to stay put while he pulled gloves and an evidence bag from the trunk of his car.

49

He worked quickly collecting evidence from the scene, and didn't stop until Lydia was already on her way to the hospital.

"Well, it seems you survived our little ordeal. There are people who have been worried about you. It might have been polite to let them know you were okay." The words were mild, but Adriel felt the rebuke.

"There were circumstances," she knew it was a lame excuse; the lift of his left eyebrow told her he felt the same. "Is everyone okay? Kat?"

"She's fine. Her trip to the other side had..." He trailed off to find the correct word. "Consequences. Or maybe perks. I guess it depends on how you look at it."

Of course; Adriel should have realized something like this could happen. Conduits to the other side are not static. They alter shapes depending on human perception. For some, the portal appears as a tunnel filled with white light; other souls preferred to cross over a bridge made from a rainbow. Still others simply floated up, or rode a boat, a white horse, or even a unicorn. Being a guardian and not a reaper, Adriel's duties lay with the living—and in policing any entity threatening mortals. Messing around with the bridge had been a desperate act, and outside her scope entirely. Kat had passed through the portal in both directions without the precautions a true reaper might have taken. In trying to cover up her original error, Adriel had thoughtlessly exposed her to backlash.

"She lost her ability to speak to the dead?"

"No, not even close."

"It increased?" Adriel's stomach flipped over; it was a sensation she found particularly unnerving. "She didn't lose her..."

"No, her vision is fine." Zack assured.

"And you? You crossed over and back as well. Did you suffer any...repercussions?"

A twist of his lips told her he had. She really didn't want to hear what he had to say. Her chances of coming out looking good were somewhere between naught and nil.

Zack huffed out a breath that was half laugh, half rueful exclamation. "Ever meet a human lie detector?"

"I'm sorry. Everything happened so quickly—I didn't think it through. Maybe I could have found another way."

"And what? Take a chance on not getting Kat back? Even if I'd known, you couldn't have stopped me going. Besides, I can think of worse gifts for a cop to have."

"I suppose." Adriel searched his eyes for the conviction of truth. He wasn't the only one with that ability, though hers had only been enhanced by her supernatural power. It was an eternity's worth of experience that had turned her into a shrewd judge of character.

"You know I'm going to have to tell them I saw you, right?"

"Yes." Adriel's eye twitched. She could have hugged him when he changed the subject.

"In the meantime, tell me what happened here."

"Something told me I needed to come outside, and to hurry. I found her on the ground—unconscious"

"You didn't move her, right?"

"I checked her pulse then ran to call for help. When I got back, I covered her with a blanket and waited for the ambulance to arrive. She remained unconscious the entire time."

Standing quietly under his scrutiny and justifying it as an omission instead of the lie it was, Adriel left out the part about using her diminished power to stabilize Lydia's condition. Zack knew her as a full angel; trying to explain her current status would have to wait until she had a better handle on it. Accessing supernatural talent to heal had raised questions she couldn't yet answer for herself—much less for him.

"Is she your next assignment?"

It was a hard question to answer. "Not technically," she offered, hoping he would let it go.

He did, but not before giving her a hard look. Adriel remembered his newfound ability to tell a lie from the truth. It shouldn't have worked on an angel, but then, she wasn't sure exactly what she was anymore—and she hadn't lied. "How well do you know the victim? Does she have any enemies?"

"I've never seen her before today. The only people I know in town are my boss and the people I work with at Just Desserts."

"Your boss? Are you an undercover angel now?" That look again. The one that made her want to squirm. Heat flared up her neck, burned her face.

"Something like that." How was she supposed to explain? Should she say she was so undercover she was human? "Speaking of my boss reminds me how late I am for work. Are we finished? I am sure I have told you everything I know."

A twist of his lips said he doubted her veracity, but other than treating him to a level look, she let it go.

"If you think of anything else, you'll call me." He made it a statement of fact rather than a question, and seemed satisfied when Adriel nodded. He handed her a card with his phone number on it. "I'll tell my sister and her friends I've seen you and you aren't dead. They won't be at all upset to learn you were nearby this whole time and never let them know." Dry sarcasm did not go unnoticed.

"Honestly, I didn't know I was still nearby, but thank you." With a graceful bow of her head, Adriel beat a hasty retreat through the waving grass while a frowning Zack watched her go. She wasn't about to tell him she had lost three months somewhere along the line. There would be too many questions for which she still had no answers.

Lost in thought, Adriel failed to notice the boy on his bike until he was nearly upon her. He looked to be about eight, or maybe ten years old, a shock of bright blond hair falling over his eyes. The bike he rode was right out of the '70s. Purple metal flake paint sparkled in the sun, and a chrome bar curved behind the elongated white seat set low behind tall, up-curved handlebars. The playing card he'd clipped on with a clothespin ticked against the spokes with each revolution of the wheel.

Speeding past, he shot her a cheeky grin before standing up on the pedals and quickly propelling himself up the hill.

She couldn't swear to it, but she thought it was the same boy from the day before.

Pam's shop nestled in the center of a short block of stores making up the commercial section of Longbrook. On one side, it was flanked by a hair salon—on the other, a larger building hosted several businesses including a real estate office, a notary public, and an attorney. Today, when she walked up to Just Desserts nearly three quarters of an hour late for her shift, Adriel found a small group of people milling around outside.

"What happened? Did you see anything? Was it a car accident? Who's hurt?"

Of course. The sound of screaming sirens had drawn attention.

Before she could address the rapid-fire of questions thrown at her, Pam swung out through the door and beckoned her inside.

"I'm late. Please accept..."

Pam waved her attempt at an apology aside. "Never mind that, tell me what happened." The small crowd followed them into the bakery.

"One of my neighbors was injured." The brief answer was not what Pam wanted to hear. She wanted a name. "Lydia Keough."

"Tell me everything."

"I went out for an early morning walk," was what Adriel meant to say. The partial truth seemed safer than complete honesty. The lie would not pass her lips. Omitting certain facts had been her stock in trade for all the centuries of time. Humans rarely ever needed or wanted complete truth, though no angel was allowed to out and out lie. Surely now she was human, Adriel was free to exercise free will and fib if she felt like it. She opened her mouth and tried again. The words stuck in her throat and would not emerge. Thinking fast, she covered, "I found her lying unconscious in the field, so I made her comfortable," an allowable partial truth, "then called for help. Zack thinks she was attacked."

"You're on a first name basis with Zack Roman?" The revelation distracted Pam for a split second. "Never mind. Is Lydia…"

"Alive. Her condition is critical. She took a hard blow to the head."

"Head injury. So someone bashed the meddling old busybody," Pam said thoughtfully. "This is going to be the biggest story since my own family tragedy; a nine day's wonder that lasted thirty years."

A family tragedy would explain those fleeting moments of sadness Adriel detected every once in a while when Pam let her defenses down. "Do you want to talk about it?"

"It's no secret. Thirty years ago this summer, my little brother, Ben, disappeared without a trace. Just like that, our lives were turned upside down and my family never really recovered."

Adriel laid a hand over Pam's, trying to communicate her sympathy with the simple touch.

Chapter Five

Halfway through Adriel's first official shift, the electronic cash register emitted a series of demented pinging noises before going dark and silent. *Oh great,* she thought, *my first day after training, and I've already broken something. What an auspicious start.*

The customer, a rather stout woman wearing a hand-knit sweater crafted from variegated yarn in shades of pink and purple unflattering to her sallow coloring, fixed Adriel with a look that plainly said she was not amused by this little blip in her day. Impatience translated into the tapping of a foot quite dainty in size compared to the rest of the woman, and only succeeded in flustering Adriel more.

It was early afternoon; Pam and Hamlin had already returned with the empty food truck, elated to have sold out in under two hours. So, when Pam pulled out a little device attached to her cell phone to read the woman's credit card, everyone breathed a sigh of relief.

"Don't worry, it happens sometimes when you bump two numbers at once." Pam shrugged off the incident and unplugged the machine. "Cutting power for a minute or two usually resets it without a problem," and sure enough, when she connected the plug, the register beeped a few more times and went back to working properly.

After the customer sailed out the door like a battleship on a mission, Pam glanced pointedly toward the plate glass window where they could see the annoyed woman easing herself into a very large, very old car and whispered, "Mrs. Donato must have gone off her diet."

Because it seemed expected, Adriel nodded and matched the knowing grin on Pam's face, but had no idea why her new boss found the prospect amusing. She might have asked, but was interrupted by Hamlin letting Pam know he had a tray ready for the case.

When the tinkling of the bell signaled another customer, Adriel squared her aching shoulders. Tired feet carried her back behind the counter where she looked up to meet the gaze of a woman in her early sixties. Thick-lensed glasses with dark frames intensified a pair of piercing dark eyes carrying a speculative expression. Shallow grooves set into a round face, framed by chin-length, time-streaked hair, evidenced she wore this particular expression often enough it had begun to leave marks in her skin. Something about her looked familiar.

"What can I get for you?"

"Who are you?" The tone carried just a hint of aggression.

"My name is Adriel. I just…I'm new here." Adriel offered no additional information since there was none to give.

"You move here with your family?"

"No, there's only me."

"Where are you staying?"

"In a cabin up the road." Adriel gestured in the general direction of the cabin. "Pam was kind enough to offer me sanctuary."

"You don't say." The woman yelled toward the rear of the bakery, "You finally found someone gullible enough to take on that nightmare and she actually thinks you're doing her a favor? Where did you find her? Rubes R Us?"

Pam never looked up from the notes she was making in a spiral bound notebook. Adriel thought her lack of response quite odd.

"It won't be a bad little house once it's cleaned up."

"House," she snorted. "That place is a hole and you can't deny it, Pamela Allen. Are you listening to me?"

Pam kept writing.

"That building should be condemned. It's not a fit place for anyone to live," the newcomer argued hotly. When her head swiveled back toward Adriel, she finally realized where she had seen that face before. It looked entirely different now, animated by strong emotion, than when Adriel had found its owner lying unconscious in the field. How could the woman have recovered so quickly?

The answer slapped Adriel in the face: she hadn't. Lydia Keough was not here in the flesh, only in spirit, and not only could Pam not see the ghost, the entire conversation was going unheard.

"I'm someone in this town, so you'd do best not to ignore me." Lydia wound up for a longer pitch.

Head swiveling like a spectator at a ping pong tournament, Adriel watched Lydia rail at Pam, who remained completely oblivious. The diatribe looked like it could go on awhile, and so when Hamlin stepped from the kitchen to call Adriel in for a break, she followed him while keeping an ear on Lydia. She didn't know what else to do.

"You want this?"

Adriel accepted the sandwich Hamlin held out to her. Keeping a straight face while Lydia resorted to a bout of colorful name calling, she plunked down on one of the stools Hamlin kept handy.

"Stinking dishrag, dirty son of a deer tick's cousin." Individually the words Lydia screamed made sense, together they sounded like nonsense.

Sweet relief for her tired feet was the only thing stopping Adriel from marching back out front and putting a stop to the yelling no one else could hear. Well, that and whatever magic substance Hamlin had put in the sandwich. She recognized bacon, tomato, and lettuce, but not the creamy condiment tasting of salt and a smoky spice to complement the bacon.

"What's in this?"

Hamlin grinned, "I make my own aioli. Eggs, oil, a little salt, and some smoked paprika."

"It's really good." Adriel closed her eyes in appreciation for the food.

***

Hamlin watched Adriel for a long moment before looking away. The way she ate mesmerized him. Chewing slowly and savoring each bite, she made him want to cook a hundred meals with exotic spices and flavors just to watch her eyes flutter closed in an ecstasy of gastronomic delight. His desire bordered on the prurient even though his motive was innocent. Or almost innocent, anyway. He wanted to feed her more than he wanted to touch her. What did that say about him?

Was the way she ate what attracted him to her the most? He wondered. Or was it her undeniable beauty? No, it was more than just looks. It was an electric grace running through her like water seeking a level place to lie.

If he had known there were occasions just like this one, when his thoughts were so precisely focused she could hear them clearly, he would have been mortified.

***

Today the poetry of his musings carried them clearly from his mind to hers, and Adriel felt like a voyeur. Why was it only Hamlin she could read without even trying? Had their near-miss experience opened up some weird channel, or was he just a natural at projecting? Since there was no solid information to work from, she decided to let it go for the time being. Chasing the rabbit down that particular hole would probably only lead to more questions than answers.

Shutting down the connection left Adriel feeling bereft. Though the last thing she wanted was to peek into his mind uninvited, those times when she was able to do so allowed her to feel more like her normal self. Still, being selfish was not

58

fair to him. Forcing her mind away, she refocused her attention on the single-minded enjoyment of the last two bites of her sandwich.

As a result, Adriel never noticed the silence—or the tinkling of the bell as Lydia passed through the door—or Pam entering the room. Consequently, both she and Hamlin jumped when a throat cleared loudly behind them.

Pam gave Hamlin's shoulder a squeeze. He quickly took the hint, grabbed his plate, and vacated the chair. In a minute, he was back with a second sandwich for his boss. Pam slid into his place at the table and began to eat. There was something odd in her manner. Something Adriel couldn't quite put her finger on.

Maybe it had to do with Lydia. "Could you tell me about the woman I found?"

"Lydia lived just up past your place. The big house on the left with all the windows."

Adriel knew the one: red brick with a pitched roof and circular driveway.

"She's dead, isn't she?" There was no need to ask, given Adriel's experience with the woman not half an hour ago, but making it a question rather than a statement of fact seemed the right thing to do.

"Yes. Word travels fast in this town; I got the call about her a few minutes ago." Despite all evidence to the contrary, Pam would miss their verbal sparring sessions. "Her husband, Ed, is a wonderful man. He was the backbone of the community until his heart attack last year. He took to his bed, and she jumped at the chance to usurp his place. She says he asked her to be his eyes and ears, but there's no way he would ever have authorized the ditch work they're doing. That's the dry side of the road, and he has always been very careful not to waste taxpayer dollars. Her death is going to have a huge impact on him. And on our town." She fiddled with a paper napkin lying next to her plate—folding and unfolding it while she waited for Adriel to say something.

"I'm sorry for your loss." Adriel sensed Pam felt more sadness than she let on.

"Yes, well, I didn't like her and I never made any secret of the fact. But someone killed her. It's official; Zack Roman is calling it murder and bringing in the Staties—State Police," Pam clarified. "Word is he is going to start questioning *persons of interest* in the case."

"And you're afraid you are going to be one of them."

"No doubt about it. We've had some spectacular fights over the years, most of them in public."

The rest of the afternoon passed in a flurry of patrons speaking in hushed, but excited tones about Lydia and the ramifications of her untimely passing.

Half an hour after stalking out the first time, Lydia herself returned to take up a seat in the corner of the room where she listened with growing horror to the inevitable escalation of fantasy in the rumors swirling around her death.

She was still there at the end of shift, and spoke only one sentence to Adriel's back as she walked out the door, "I know what you are, and now I'm yours."

***

How was she supposed to help Lydia with blocked powers? All the signs were there: feeling sorry for herself, descending into a pit of why-me thinking, and petulance— Adriel was in the midst of a pity party. Any one of her former charges would testify to her lack of patience with those types of soirées, and yet, she couldn't seem to shake it.

In all the hullabaloo, she had forgotten about her charges. Little Beatrice, who lived in foster care and despaired of ever finding a family to call her own. Who would the collective send to help Beatrice? Surely not Calamiel. His gruff manner and deep voice erred on the side of too stern. Maybe Hamith? No, she was good with kids, but something of a pushover. Beatrice needed a strong hand to keep her in line. Three sets of prospective parents had already caught her on bad days, and missed seeing the bright spirit bubbling under the prickly armor of her exterior.

And what about Amethyst? Her transformation to full reader had not come with an instruction manual. She would need guidance to use her elevated abilities, or they could backfire and cause repercussions in the future.

Winston's soft purr couldn't pull Adriel out of the funk she was in. If she could only go home; even a short visit would recharge her batteries. Never had she felt so depleted.

"Estelle. I need you," Adriel called out into the silence. "Please, I need to go home." Winston, now only feigning sleep, watched through slitted eyes as Adriel sank to her knees on the floor—pounding against it with sharp blows until she was spent, her hands bruised and torn.

Adriel huddled there on the weathered wood, amid the smell of her own blood mixed with the dry powdery dust, and tried to recapture the sense of rightness she had felt in the past. No matter how hard she tried to find it, peace remained as distant as a purple mountain horizon.

Estelle couldn't tell an outright lie. So, she must have been wrong. There was no such thing as an earthbound angel—a divine being in fleshly form. It was impossible.

Don't be so sure about that, a voice whispered over the silence. The sound of Adriel's heartbeat rushing through her ears reminded her of the soft rustle her wings once made. Instead of comfort, the memory brought more pain.

Thinking sleep would be her best form of escape, Adriel levered up off the floor, her body moving like it had aged a hundred years. She threaded her way through the wall of boxes to settle down on the bed, where her head was still sinking into the pillow's softness as she fell into dreaming. A rapid-fire series of images rolled past—highlights of time spent in service to both man and the divine.

A million lifetimes passed by before dreamtime slowed to a crawl to show her the moments when the food truck bore down with certain death. Her perspective doubled until she was both experiencing the near miss and watching it from the outside. From the distant vantage point she saw the truck start to slide. Simple physics predicted there was no way that many tons of rolling metal could stop in time. So what had happened?

Closer and closer the truck skidded. Adriel watched her own hands lift in what should have been a futile effort to stave off the collision. When the subtle wave of power flowed from the dream Adriel to alter the bounds of reality and bring the truck to a stop, the sleeping Adriel saw what Hamlin and Pam had seen in that moment. Not adrenaline-fueled wishful thinking, but a true vision of a beam of light and the shadow of wings.

The same beam and shadow hovered when she watched her dream self lay hands on Lydia.

It was enough of a shock to startle Adriel fully awake.

Adriel raised both hands, turned them over to search them intently. She had no idea what to look for, since angel powers left no trace. All she saw were smears of dried blood.

Closing her eyes, she reached for the power that once pooled at the seat of her grace. She pictured her hands clean and unbroken; all traces of her emotional upheaval wiped away. She imagined the familiar feeling of connecting to the energy flowing through the universe—the sensation of shaping that energy, directing it to suit the need.

Like a radio station incorrectly tuned, a short burst of energetic static proved her connection was tenuous, but still present. Maybe all was not lost.

Hope snapped Adriel's eyes open, lifted her hands slowly to where she could see what, if any, healing effect had occurred. The smears of dried blood still decorated her milky skin.

She growled in frustration, because the way to the bathroom was blocked again by a stack of boxes moved there during a recent bout of sorting. When she finally reached the sink to run trembling hands under the water, her breath caught and held while the blood sluiced down the drain to reveal pink skin and days-old scabs where freshly torn wounds had been.

A prayer of thanks arrowed homeward, elation flooded through every molecule of her being until she felt filled to the brim with hope. If she could bend energy to stop a truck, and at least partially heal her own skin, this earthbound angel thing might not be so bad after all.

Maybe there was a way she could go home.

***

"You cheated," Estelle accused Julius. "She didn't do that all on her own."

"Best way to push through a block is to believe you can. She fails, we fail—they made that point quite clear, as you well know. All I did was give her a nudge."

"I'm surrounded by renegades."
***
Right in the middle of deciding what the next test of her powers would be, Adriel was interrupted by the persistent sound of someone kicking at the door.

"Adriel, open up. Hurry." Pam's voice sounded muffled and strange.

When the door swung open, it was easy to see why. A single eye skewered Adriel from behind an armload of paper grocery bags filled to overflowing. Pam staggered toward the kitchen area, only to find the passage too narrow to fit through. From too far away, Adriel watched one of the bags tilt, a carton of eggs sliding toward the edge of no return. She lunged but would have come up an inch short if, without a second thought, she hadn't bent energy enough to pull the bag toward her through the air.

Even with the second bag partially obscuring her vision, Pam felt something odd. After dumping the bag on the table, she rested hands on her hips, tilted her head back, and eyed Adriel with suspicion.

"Close call." Adriel turned her face away and called over her shoulder as she set the bag on the counter. Because it seemed prudent, she busied herself with sorting through its contents in order to avoid meeting Pam's curious gaze. She was just putting a carton of eggs into the cabinet when Pam snatched it from her hand and deposited it in the refrigerator.

"Not had much experience in the kitchen?" There was a sardonic edge to the question, and Adriel had no defense.

"It shows?"

"A bit." Pam nudged Adriel aside to rescue several other perishables from the cabinet shelf before relegating them to cold storage. "Good way to contract food poisoning. How did you get to be an adult and not know milk has to be kept cold?"

"I might have led a sheltered life, but that doesn't make me a pampered twit."

Embarrassment flamed Pam's cheeks a vivid red. "I never said any such thing."

"Well, you were thinking it," Adriel snapped.

"So what? You read people's thoughts now?"

Had she? Hamlin's thoughts occasionally made it past the block, but only at random. Adriel paled and slapped a hand over her mouth. Above her hand, wide eyes turned to meet Pam's openly curious gaze.

"All right, " Pam said. "Out with it. Whatever it is you're hiding, it can't be worse than what I'll imagine if you don't tell me."

"Oh, I think it can." An intensely vivid image of being fitted for one of those lovely white coats with the sleeves that fastened in the back played through Adriel's mind. "Trust me, you wouldn't believe me if I told you the truth."

"Try me." Voice colder than a mud puddle in January, Pam deadpanned, "You might be surprised."

Burdening Pam with such an enormous secret without counting the possible cost would be extremely irresponsible. Still, her history of telling alternate versions of the truth—okay, fine, outright lies if you want to be picky about it—had met with mixed success. Who knew what might come out of her mouth if she opened it.

Winston saved her from the attempt by choosing that precise moment to launch from his perch on top of the refrigerator to the counter and then, by way of Pam's shoulder, to the table. His claws dug in long enough to leave angry red marks on tender flesh while she hurled several imaginative names at him. Being a typical cat, he ignored Pam as thoroughly as he groomed the back of his leg, and with the same amount of concentration.

By the time her ire was spent, Pam had forgotten all about whatever secret Adriel might be hiding, and Winston did not wink at Adriel. Probably not.

Chapter Six

Muscles bunching under sleek black fur, Winston leapt straight up to land heavily on the tallest stack of boxes. Adriel sucked in a breath when she saw the tower wobble. "Nooo," her voice sounded loud in the room. "No. No. No." Bad enough she had signed on to sort through this mess, she didn't fancy cleaning up some domino pile of trash because of a crazy cat with no respect for the laws of gravity.

She wagged a finger in the cat's face, "Cute will only get you so far with me, mister." His sarcastic answer was to send his sandpaper tongue rasping across fur as he shot a hind leg into the air to clean it of dirt particles invisible to the naked eye. Once or twice, he paused to give her a look of disdain. "Just remember, I control the kibble." Relenting, Adriel gave him a scratch under the chin.

Talking to animals was a pleasure Adriel missed. Their bright chatter charmed her every time. Either Winston was unnaturally quiet, or her ability to hear animals had gone the way of her wings. Sad thought.

"This one?" Adriel pointed to a medium-sized box and cocked her head toward Winston, who soundly ignored the question. "Fine, this one it is." A steak knife made short work of the tape holding the box closed. "I hope there are no body parts in here." Still talking to the cat, Adriel flipped the flaps open to sneak a peek inside. With a languid stretch, Winston slithered over to peer down from his perch and satisfy his own curiosity.

Dirty socks.

At least six months' worth. Their fragrance perfumed the air with a musty funk nasty enough to bring tears to her eyes. Not a dead body, though it smelled nearly as bad. Why in the world would someone fill a box with their filthy laundry? It defied logic.

Dumping them in the washer sounded like a good idea. Unless adding water might intensify the stench. Instead, Adriel rifled through the cupboards for tape to seal the box back up, and a pen to mark the contents on the outside. Pam's instructions did not cover this particular contingency, and there was only so far Adriel was willing to go to ensure a roof over her head. Handling foul footwear went way over the line.

"Should we open another?" Again, Winston declined to answer, so Adriel pulled the next box from the pile and slit open the tape. When the flaps came free, she held her breath, just in case.

Not dirty laundry this time. Nope. This box was filled to the brim with plastic forks; clean, and still in their original boxes. She marked, sealed, and set it aside. There was something addictive about the activity, and with curiosity running rampant, she grabbed a little box from another pile.

Inside were six smaller boxes labeled Pet Rock. "Pet Rock? I bet the only trick it does is roll over and play dead." She pulled one of them out to inspect more thoroughly. Nestled in a bed of straw lay a small gray rock attached to a silver chain, and a booklet defining its proper care and feeding. Leafing through the tiny pamphlet, it became clear the whole concept of a pet rock was an attempt at humor.

She might be one of them now, but without doubt, humans were weird.

***

Lydia's murder was still the topic of conversation during Adriel's third ever shift at Just Desserts. Today, though, no one was in a big hurry to leave, not even when the cash register coughed and died for the third time.

A pro at it now, Adriel reached down to pull the plug while she chatted with the customer.

Once the tinkling bell quieted, Pam called Adriel into the back where lunch plates waited on the table for them both. "Wiletta, handle the front, please," she called, and then to Adriel said, "Have you found anything interesting in Craig's boxes?"

Half in humor and half in disgust, Adriel answered, "Dirty socks, plastic utensils and Pet Rocks."

"Dirty socks?" Pam shook her head then folded her elbows on the table to cradle her face in her hands.

"Those are the items I found this morning."

Behind them, Hamlin, who had been quietly icing cupcakes and listening intently to every word, snorted.

"Smelly ones." Adriel added, with the beginnings of a smirk. The absurdity of collecting stinky undergarments in a box had seemed bizarre to her at first; now it was flat out funny. The smirk turned to a smile and then to a small snort of laughter. "I'm beginning to feel like an archaeologist on a dig, uncovering ancient civilizations and trying to guess why they chose this or that shape for their pots."

"I wish I could say Uncle Craig only started hoarding when his memory began to fail, but it would be a lie. There are boxes in there with things that probably haven't seen the light of day in almost thirty years. He always was a bit odd."

Now Adriel felt bad for laughing about the socks.

"Listen, forget about room and board, the cabin is yours for as long as you want it. I'm going to start paying you hourly for your work here, and I'll even help you with the cleaning and painting in my spare time." More than embarrassment over the dirty socks motivated Pam. Spending time with Adriel was starting to feel a bit like having a friend. A thing sadly lacking in her life.

With that settled, Pam's expression turned uncertain; her eyes met Adriel's, slid away then back, "May I ask you something personal?"

"You may, and if I can, I will answer."

There was no way to ask delicately, so Pam just blurted out, "You don't have any other clothes, do you?"

The question hit Adriel from out of nowhere. She missed how easily she used to change her appearance with nothing more than a thought. Not just hair and eye color, but height, weight, and yes, clothes, too. She had never owned clothing, hence there had been none to leave behind. Nor any to bring along even if she'd gotten advance notice of her change in status.

"I have no possessions." Adriel confirmed Pam's suspicions. "Given the way we met, it must be obvious."

"That's it then." Pam's vehemence flipped Adriel's stomach like a pancake. Was she going to be fired over a lack of alternate wardrobe? "I'm giving you an advance on your pay, and after your shift is over, we're going shopping." Pam was already looking forward to it.

"And the dirty socks? What shall I do with those?"

"I'll take them." Hamlin offered, and when Pam gave him a questioning look, said, "I know the homeless shelters don't accept used underwear, but there's no reason I can't drop a box of clean socks down on Canal Street where those who need them will find them. That way they won't go to waste."

Pam made a quick phone call to arrange for a trash company to drop off a portable dumpster at the cabin for items like the plastic cutlery no one would ever want to use. Everything else, she decided, could be sorted and donated, or sold.

Adriel spent the rest of the day trying to find an excuse to call off the shopping expedition.

***

"We don't have to do this. I can just wash these garments each night. It's been working for me so far. They're perfectly serviceable." Okay, maybe the underwear pinched a little when the standard outfit for this persona had gone from being corporeal to physical—there were worse things to endure.

"You can't come to work in the same clothes every day. People will talk."

"About my clothes?" Why on earth would anyone care about that? "Surely there are better topics of conversation."

"You would think." A wry smile twisted the corners of Pam's mouth. The shadow passing through her eyes told Adriel the other woman had experience with being the target of gossip. "And yet, they will."

No matter how hard Adriel tried to fit into her new life, she doubted she would ever understand this particular aspect of humans. The fascination with judging people from the outside-in seemed ridiculous to her. In the past, she had taken on many forms in order to better communicate with her charges. Yet, under each of those various guises, the person inside remained the same. The angel Galmadriel. Nothing more, nothing less. The outer package was nothing more than window dressing for the soul inside.

"Besides," Pam continued, giving Adriel a head to toe appraisal, "You're already bringing me in some new clientele—of the male persuasion—once word gets around town, more of them will show up to check you out. They'll look, and they'll buy donuts, and sandwiches, and coffee. I figure it's an investment in my business."

Seeing herself beaten, Adriel gave in. It wasn't like she had much of a choice, anyway. When Pam made up her mind, she was hard to dissuade. That didn't mean Adriel was looking forward to the experience. Pam was, though. With a grin like she'd found a fourteenth donut in her baker's dozen, she dragged Adriel to the car and started reciting a laundry list of needed items. By the time they got to the mall, Adriel's head was starting to pound. From the sounds of things, Pam was about to turn her into a real life Barbie doll. Adriel sensed Pam hadn't had a lot of friends growing up, and was trying hard to make up for lost time.

Once in the mall, Pam was like a steamroller on a mission, and Adriel had to step lively to keep up with her.

"First stop, Underlings." Pam appraised the body before her shrewdly. "We'll get you a bra fitting."

Had Adriel known what one would entail, she would have fought tooth and nail to keep from being pulled through the shop door. Two steps inside, she fell into the clutches of a woman named Rona, who reminded her of a dark-haired Marilyn Monroe. At first, Adriel made the mistake of underestimating Rona. A soft spoken order to follow her into the back, while she plucked a series of undergarments from various racks along the way had Adriel thinking this whole experience might not be so bad. Once parked in front of a three way mirror, though, everything changed. Rona went from sweet shop mistress to drill sergeant at roughly half the speed of light, and before Adriel could utter the first word of protest, she was buck naked to the waist. With no sense of propriety whatsoever, Rona reached around Adriel from the back and buckled her into what looked like a torture device of a bra. It had wires in it, for crying out loud.

"Bend over and shake the girls into place." Rona ordered.

"Girls?" At first Adriel didn't realize Rona meant her breasts. Once she had shimmied and jiggled to Rona's satisfaction, she was mortified when the proprietor proceeded to further adjust the fit of the garment—by reaching right into the bra to handle the girls like she owned them. Shock silenced any rebuke Adriel could dredge up.

"There. It looks great." A tweak to one of the straps. "How does it feel?"

It was the first time being allowed any input, and Adriel couldn't form a single sentence. There she was, decked out in a lace-edged, tartan-print bra that felt surprisingly comfortable despite the garish colors and wires; mouth hanging open, and facing her wide-eyed reflection staring back from three different directions. Rona gave her a little nudge.

"Move around a little, tell me if it binds anywhere." Scarlet-tipped hands guided Adriel through a series of movements designed to test the fit.

"I…it feels fine. Does it come in something less…vivid?" Adriel fingered the lace edge that was already starting to itch. "Maybe without the lace?"

"Of course. This whole line is on clearance with a BOGO. I'll bring you some more options. Meantime, try this one," she tossed a satin number at Adriel's head and bustled out of the curtained enclosure. To keep the manhandling to a minimum, Adriel hurriedly shrugged into the second bra and adjusted everything before Rona returned.

"Those are nice, which one is clearance and which is BOGO?" To her credit, the buxom shop owner never cracked a smile when she explained Adriel could get two bras for the price of one, and at a reduced price. Adriel launched a short war of the wills over narrowing her choices to two, in subdued colors most suited to her sensibilities, then exited the changing room to find Pam brandishing a handful of something called thongs in the air.

"What do you think? Sexy, right?"

Adriel's confusion must have been written clearly on her face, because Pam dropped the rest and held one up the way it was meant to be worn.

"That's indecent. If I'm seeing this correctly, the strap is going to go right between…" a rush of blood stained Adriel's cheeks with embarrassed red. She had already experienced the annoyance of the wedgie phenomenon, and had no intention of willingly subjecting herself to it again. Besides, she had no use for being sexy.

"You won't feel a thing. They're very comfortable."

She treated Rona's statement with the scorn it deserved, and put her foot firmly down on the whole topic of a handful of straps doubling as panties.

The next store Pam dragged her into had better be less traumatizing, or she was out of there. Moving along in Pam's wake, Adriel caught the scent of freshly-brewed coffee.

Instinctively, her nose turned toward the dark, rich miasma and the rest of her followed it right up to the counter where she got the chance to place an order for something called a Macchiato before Pam noticed her absence. Amused, Adriel watched Pam backtrack, her feet tapping out a staccato on the tile floors.

"Sorry, I needed sustenance."

Pam arched an eyebrow. "It'll take more than that to keep up with me. We'd better hit the food court first."

"Food court? Is that where Burger King rules?"

"That's not even a little bit funny."

"Then why are you smiling?"

"Because you're ridiculous." Compliment or insult? At times, Adriel had trouble knowing the difference.

"No more underwear." It was a warning and an order gloved in a smile.

Pam held up her hands in a gesture of surrender about as genuine as a silicone implant. It, combined with the gleam of amusement in her eye, inspired zero trust in the purity of her motives. Adriel decided to turn the tables.

"Maybe you could do with a wardrobe spruce. I'm sure Rona has time to give you a fitting." That wiped the smile off Pam's face. "Give your girls a lift." Revealing a talent for mimicry she nailed Rona's breathy vocal delivery.

"A dress. Let's go pick you out something pretty." With a speed borne of practice, Pam swept the empty coffee containers from the elevated bistro table. Several doors down they passed a shop advertising brand name clothing at discounted prices. When Pam would have passed right by, Adriel redirected her inside.

Modestly dressed herself, Pam's choices for Adriel were anything but. Cotton sundresses that bared arms, shoulders, and legs were not Adriel's style. Fifteen minutes flew past while Adriel established parameters for what she considered acceptable.

74

"What's wrong with this?" Pam held up a floral number featuring a fitted bodice with a deep V neck. "See, no spaghetti straps." She fingered the narrow-cut shoulder.

"It's not decent."

"I'd wear it if I had the bod. On me it would look like a sack draped over a pile of potatoes."

"It would not. You have lovely, strong shoulders." Adriel turned it back on Pam, "You're a young woman still. Why don't you try a little color in your wardrobe. Drab gray doesn't fit your nature."

"Hah, lot you know. I'm forty-three. That's middle aged, not young."

"Forty is the new thirty." Adriel intoned. She'd read it on the cover of a magazine and not really understood what it meant until now.

Two exhausting hours later, the pair stumbled back out carrying several bags between them. Adriel now owned the basics of a mix and match wardrobe. What's more, she had even managed to talk Pam into buying a few things for herself.

Exiting from the cool mall atmosphere, the blast of hot, humid air felt like walking into a sauna. Tendrils of hair plastered themselves to Adriel's neck and face. The walk to the Jeep took them close enough to hear an argument in process. Voices raised to a strident level echoed off the partially enclosed parking structure's walls. Pam signaled for Adriel to stop. Adriel's keen hearing picked up the conversation from where she stood.

"Don't threaten me; I know where all your skeletons are buried, too. Or did you tell your wife about your night with..." the rest was a bit garbled, but it sounded like he said Miss Terry Dancing Pants.

"Leave my wife out of it. If I had any proof of what you did, I'd..."

"You'd do well to be careful about threatening me."

The two men passed out of hearing range.

"Those voices sounded familiar," Pam kept playing the conversation back in her head. "With the echo in here, I can't be certain."

"It's a big mall, it could have been anyone from anywhere. It's none of our business," But Adriel filed the sounds away in her memory.

Chapter Seven

Through slow and steady progress, the number of boxes in the cabin had been reduced by a quarter—not counting the boxes on the far side of the porch. Hamlin's dirty socks count continued to increase. So far, he had cleaned three trash bags full and dropped them off where they would be found and used by folks who needed them.

Trying to see the glass as half full, Adriel decided she was glad the man had not collected dirty underpants the same way he did his dirty socks. Two boxes of blankets and a box of coats, though, were happily accepted by Hamlin's friend and distributed to the shelter. Craig's castoffs were going to good use.

Over the last couple of days, though, box sorting had slowed down in favor of getting certain outside projects done. Using Callum's trick, Adriel replaced every broken shingle on the outside of the little cabin. After sweeping down more cobwebs than she had ever seen in one place, she sorted through the contents of the small attached shed behind the cabin to find rakes, hoes, a scythe, and an old-fashioned, rotary push mower.

Pushing the beast a mere two feet through overgrown grass was enough to send Adriel back to the shed for the scythe. Oiled and sharpened before it had been stored, it's blade snicked and sliced with each swing until her upper arms burned and she was forced to take a break. After half an hour of hard slog, she despaired over having cleared hardly any of the area she intended to mow.

Adriel rotated her shoulders to ease the ache, then lifted the long, curling mass of hair off her neck to let the light breeze brush damp sweat into coolness. This whole mowing business needed a rethink. At this rate, it would take weeks to get the lawn into shape. Her scalp felt tender from the sun's burning heat, and when she caught sight of herself in the mirror, she realized her nose and cheeks had also reddened from its fiery touch.

Sunblock. There had been a tube of it in the medicine cabinet, and now she remembered reading what it was for. SPF-50 still seemed like another language to her, but she slathered it liberally on her face and arms. The idea of rubbing the slightly greasy cream into her hair caused a shudder. No way. Too messy.

Working quickly, she plaited the mass into a single braid, then with a sigh pulled the top off the box of hats waiting in the corner for Hamlin, and pulled out a ball cap with *I'd rather be sleeping* embroidered across the front.

Actually, the saying seemed most appropriate.

Half an hour later, she had gotten into a rhythm with the scythe, and found a way to swing it less taxing on her shoulders. With body occupied, her mind was free to wander.

And where it wandered was the one place she had been doing her best not to think about. Home. Just as the aching sadness began to fill her, a sound floated across the air; one she had heard before.

Tick, tick, tick.

A playing card flicking past each spoke of a bicycle wheel.

She looked up to see the towheaded boy who had ridden by on the day of Lydia's accident. This time when he got close enough, Adriel waved.

The boy's hand came up to wave back and with eyes wide, he dumped his bike right at the end of her driveway. She raced to his side.

Before she could reach down to help him, he scrambled to his feet and pointed at her. "You waved to me," he accused.

"Yes, was I not supposed to?" Mortals had so many rules.

"And now you're talking to me."

"Sorry. I had no idea there was a rule against speaking to children."

Ben took her uncertainty for anger.

"I'm not supposed to talk to strangers, but if you tell me your name, we'll be friends?"

"Adriel. And yours?" The boy was charming and naive.

"I'm Ben. You got a funny name," he observed.

"Why thank you." She injected a bit of sarcasm into her voice; charming only went so far.

"Sorry, Miss Adriel. Mom used to say I had the manners of a goat." His cheeky grin was tinged with a sadness that puzzled Adriel almost as much as his suggestion that goats were unmannered creatures, when she had always found them to be quite civilized.

"Would you like to tell me about your family?" The grin he flashed only quivered a little around the edges.

"My mom and dad were really nice. They read me stories and tucked me in at night. Mom never made me eat all my carrots." A tear trembled on his bottom lash. "Then one day I was riding my bike and something bad happened. I saw this really, really bright light. I was scared of the light, so I went home. Everyone was crying, but nobody would tell me why. I must have been a very bad boy because Mommy stopped reading me stories, and no one ever tucked me in again."

The truth hit Adriel like a wrecking ball.

"Oh Ben, you must have been so frightened." It was now up to Adriel to explain a very complicated concept to this young boy. "Can you tell me what you remember about the bad thing that happened?"

He seemed so small, so fragile, all she wanted to do was pull him into a hug; something she could easily have done in her full angel form, but probably not in her present state.

"I was riding my bike right over there," he pointed toward the road between the cabin and Lydia's house. "A car pulled up behind me, so I moved over like Daddy showed me. Then I got a headache and I didn't feel so good. After a little while, I saw the bright light, and then I went home."

Ben's next sentence put the final twist on Adriel's heart.

"Now, new people live in my house and I can't find my mom and dad. I think something funny happened, because the last time I saw them, they looked different. You know—with gray hair and stuff. I can't go home anymore, so I just ride my bike every day. No one ever talks to me. Well, until you."

How was she supposed to explain to this bright-eyed child he was a spirit who should have crossed over a long time ago?

"Ben, do you know what it means when something dies?"

"I'm not a baby. I've seen plenty of dead animals in the road, and my grandma died when her heart attacked her."

Kid logic.

"When a person dies, the angel who comes to help them cross over sometimes looks like a bright light."

"Does that mean," Ben's mouth fell open, "I'm dead?"

"Yes. I'm afraid it does."

"I'm a ghost. Like Casper. That's why no one would talk to me. Because I'm invisible. That's so cool."

Expecting tears, Adriel was taken aback by the boy's awed tone. Maybe he was just relieved at finally knowing what had happened to him.

"Can you tell me more about the day you saw the light?"

Ben sighed.

"I was riding my bike; I got a headache; I saw the light. That's all I remember."

"Think back; did you hear anything?"

"Already told you. There was a car coming, so I moved over into the grass on the side of the road. Then, I got the headache, saw the light, pushed my bike out of the ditch, and went home."

Gently, Adriel suggested, "I think the car must have hit you."

Ben closed his eyes, his face screwed into a thoughtful expression. He nodded a couple times while it all fell into place. His eyes popped wide open.

"You're right; I remember now. I heard the car coming up fast, so I moved over into the grass and pedaled real slow. The engine got louder, so I turned around and saw this big round headlight right before I flew into the ditch."

"Did you see what kind of car it was? Or the driver?"

"Just the big round headlight and a shiny bumper. Adriel, can I ask you a question?" At her nod, Ben asked, "Do you think my mom and dad died and went into the light? You know, because they're not here anymore."

Based on what he had told her earlier, it was a possibility.

"I'll tell you what: you tell me your last name, and I'll see if I can find out for you. I'm new in town, so I don't know all the families here yet."

Before he answered, Ben had one more question of his own. "Can I still go there? Into the light, I mean. If my parents are in there, I could see them again," his voice sounded so plaintive Adriel's heart hurt for him.

His question was more complicated than he knew, for reasons she could not share.

"I think so, but it might take a little time to arrange the details. I'll do everything I can to help you."

"Okay, my last name is Allen."

A name Adriel did recognize. She should have put it together the minute she realized Ben was dead. She had just spent half an hour chatting with Pam's long lost brother, and now he was looking up at her with no idea of the thoughts racing through her mind or that she now faced the dilemma of what to tell his older sister.

Why was everything so complicated? On the one hand, Pam would be thrilled to learn what happened to her little brother; but on the other, there was no way Adriel could give her the information without sounding like a complete lunatic.

***

81

With Lydia gone, the group of citizens opposed to the new ditch renewed their efforts to get the town to put a stop to the job. By their logic, with the work half done, half the money could go back into the town coffers to be spent on more important things—necessary things. Fear of Lydia's sharp-tongued displeasure no longer a factor, the group quickly doubled in size. It was a hot topic for debate over the coffee and pastries Adriel served on her days in the bakery, until something happened that made for an even better story.

"Did you hear anything?" Pam fired the question at Adriel the second she walked through the door. Adriel's expression was all the answer she needed. "I guess that's a no. Someone poured sand into the gas tanks of every piece of ditch digging equipment last night."

It was news to Adriel. The culprit must have been very quiet.

"I guess I slept right through it, because I didn't hear a thing." Joy. A respite from the incessant hooting and banging. Okay, that was just mean, but she didn't care. "Why would anyone do a thing like that?"

"To make a point about how ridiculous it is to spend money and time on spurious projects? There's a group of us still arguing for it to be filled in and done with. I can't believe anyone in the group would jeopardize our position by taking things this far, though. Maybe it was teenagers pulling a prank."

"Does that kind of thing happen a lot?" Adriel made a beeline for the coffee station. At home, she was still at war with the coffee maker from hell, and had switched to a morning cup of tea most days. Even she couldn't screw up dunking a tea bag in a cup of hot water. Getting a decent caffeine fix either meant playing mad scientist with the coffeemaker or walking to town.

"No, not really. Our kids aren't perfect angels by any means, but in a small community like this, malicious vandalism is rare."

"What do you think will happen now? With the ditch digging, I mean." Adriel came down firmly on the side of everyone else who opposed the digging. Not for the same reasons, since she had no stake in the financial side of things, but so what?

"I can answer that," Damien Oliver spoke up. Adriel hadn't noticed him sitting quietly at a corner table. "Someone's gonna have to go up there and drain the gas out of every piece of equipment, then they're going to have to flush all the tanks and drain the lines. They only started up one of the rigs before Gideon figured out what happened. Take a couple days at most to have them all back on the job. Anyone who knows anything about vehicles would have taken a pair of snips to the wiring harness. Devil of a job to trace that kind of thing back to the source."

"Who do you think might have done it?" Adriel was curious to hear his opinion, but all she got out of him was a shrug of indifference before he hustled out the door leaving the exact change for his meal on the table. Damien wasn't much of a tipper.

"The list of people who might want to stop the work is longer than the list of people who want it to go forward. It's a pretty big pool to fish in, but I can't picture anyone taking things this far." Worry furrowed Pam's brow.

It might have been a leap, but Adriel voiced an errant thought, "Seems to me they went a lot farther than that."

Pam frowned until she caught the implication, then her eyes shot wide in shock, "Are you saying you think Lydia's death might be connected to the vandalism?"

Shrugging, Adriel replied, "It's a stretch, but I can't help thinking someone is deeply invested in stopping the ditch from being dug."

Head tilted, Pam considered. "A stretch?" Skepticism dripped from her lips, "One that would take a rubber band the size of Texas. Lydia had plenty of enemies. Not that I can picture any of them actually killing her. Or it having anything to do with this ditch."

"Maybe," but Adriel wasn't convinced.

***

Several days of silence while the machines were repaired gave Adriel the opportunity to catch up on her sleep. When they started back up again bright and early on Monday morning, she heaved a resigned sigh and wandered into the kitchen to glare at her nemesis.

The coffee maker was evil. There was no doubt in her mind as she squared off against it again. Fully half of the time, the product it produced was absolutely undrinkable. Precisely measuring the grounds and water each time made little difference in the random results. The paper filters were flimsy at best, and tore at the gentlest touch. Using two of them for added stability only made the coffee taste worse. Twice, before she abandoned the infernal machine in favor of walking to town to nip into Just Desserts, the drip area somehow became plugged with grounds. Before she could stop it, the basket overflowed and dumped a gritty mess all over the counter.

Between the trouble with it; the cell phone that dumped its charge twice a day, alternated between no service and calling itself three times a day; and the cash register at Just Desserts, she was beginning to suspect she had some sort of negative effect on electronics.

Regardless, she wanted coffee and she wanted it now. Running through a mental checklist, Adriel filled the reservoir with water. She checked the basket for stray grounds and inserted a clean filter. Moving carefully, she added scoops of ground coffee, making sure the filter stayed firmly in place. Everything seemed in order, so she closed the lid, hit the button, and walked away in case her proximity really was a factor. Burbling sounds echoed across the room just ahead of the scent. It smelled right this time. A good sign. When the machine beeped to signal it was done, she poured a cup, doctored it up the way she liked it, and took a tentative sip.

Joy, it was passable. Maybe she wasn't totally hopeless in the kitchen. Cheered by the thought, she made a plan to test out one of the recipes in those books she'd found.

Given the prospect of finding more boxes full of underthings—whether dirty or clean—she eyed the room with a certain amount of trepidation. Still, the job had to be done, so armed with a box cutter and a can-do attitude, she took stock. Boxes of every shape and size, from plastic storage bins to shoe boxes were stacked haphazardly to form the walls and partitions of a complicated maze.

Or, were they? Adriel flipped back through the photographic memory—one of the perks she had retained from being an angel. Able to picture the room exactly as it had been before she moved anything, she realized there might have been a pattern. Clearly Craig had not used box size as a criteria for choosing what went where, since larger boxes sometimes sat on a group of smaller ones. It looked, instead, as though he might have sorted them by weight or importance.

She couldn't hold back a sigh. His organizational method had zero bearing on how she should proceed, even if trying to figure it out was an interesting puzzle. It was time to stop dithering around and get to work.

Picking a stack at random, she selected the smallest box on top of the pile closest to the bedroom door, and carried it to the table to open. Winston leapt from his perch on the refrigerator to rub his cheek against the cardboard corner.

"You like this one?" Adriel asked the cat, who only purred in response. She applied blade to tape. "Well, of course you do." The box contained an assortment of kitty toys. Fast as lightning, the cat nipped out a feather-covered ball with an agile paw. A quick flick sent the ball flying across the room— the bell inside jingling madly as a blur of black fur engaged in a wild game of ball hockey snaking through the maze of boxes until he passed out of Adriel's line of sight.

A muted thump was the only warning she heard before a short stack of boxes tumbled behind the streaking cat. This must have been the reason for boxing up his toys. She set Winston's things aside and grabbed the first of three identical boot boxes left in his wake. Each was filled with balls of crumpled newsprint protecting a single item cocooned in bubble wrap and packing tape. Layers and layers of packing tape which, when carefully cut away revealed…three perfectly ordinary acorns—one in each box.

Craig's reason for collecting them defied comprehension. Though Adriel had to admit, there was a certain amount of fancy in the idea of preserving memories with such small specimens of nature. Fancy brought with it a sense of sadness over the way time or disease had eventually robbed Craig of even these small reminders. She sent out a prayer for him to find peace.

Then she sent out one for herself to find patience. Respectful though she might want to be, opening box after box full of inane items was going to test the boundaries of her patience and her sense of humor. The acorns did not go out with the trash, she lined them up on one of the shelves to remind herself within absurdity, sometimes something profound existed.

The rest of the boxes Winston had knocked down were heavy ones filled with newspapers dating from the past few years. She scanned a couple before realizing it would be a week before she finished reading those, and put them down to move on to start the next stack.

Less interesting, this section held boxes full of empty grocery bags, deli containers with no lids, lids with no containers—none of them matching—and other similar items which Adriel duly sorted. Anything recyclable—according to the list held to the refrigerator with a magnet—she set aside for that purpose. What few usable items she found were mostly clothing. Some would go to Hamlin for distribution to the homeless; the rest Craig might still be able to wear. Books, dishes, and personal items she set aside for Pam. Useless items, those being the bulk of what she found, went into the portable dumpster out front. The best find so far was a box of brightly colored pillows. Tossed onto the sofa, they cheered the room considerably.

An hour or so later, Adriel lifted the hair off her neck with a grimy hand. One more box to go. Clearing this stack meant no more dodging sideways to get from the sofa into the bedroom. A small victory.

A puff of dust swirled into the air at her sigh when, even after tugging with every ounce of her strength, the last box proved too heavy to lift. She squatted to slice at the tape holding it closed. More dust flew as she opened the flaps to find it stuffed to the brim with spiral bound notebooks, each with a date written on the front. It felt like an invasion of privacy at first, but since it was her job to sort through these items, she went ahead and flipped open the red cover of the one on top. Carefully inscribed lines formed a grid on each page where Craig had kept a chronicle of weather conditions at morning, noon, and night for an entire year.

What was she supposed to do with this type of thing? Laying the first book aside, she leafed through the next: a set of meticulous records detailing everything from his daily food intake to how many hours of sleep he had gotten the night before. When she came to the part where he noted in-depth information about his bathroom habits, she slammed the book shut.

It was a little sad to think about what might compel a man to keep notes about every minute detail of his day. Adriel was still not sure she fully understood what made mortals tick at the best of times; this was totally beyond her comprehension. She mulled it over while transferring the notebooks into two of the now-empty plastic totes and slid them under the bed. The ones marked Journal on the cover she left on top, in case Pam wanted to read them later. But for now, out of sight, out of mind.

Chapter Eight

The last person—if person was the proper term for a ghost—Adriel expected to hear calling her through the screen door was Lydia. A quick calculation put the woman five days in the grave; a bit late for her to still be hanging around. *Just what I need*, Adriel thought, *another ghost with unfinished business.* Didn't anyone just cross over anymore? Lydia's eyes widened when they met Adriel's. This was no eight-year-old boy, too young to fully grasp the concept of an afterlife. Last time the two had spoken, Lydia had been brand-spanking dead; this time, though, she knew the score. Adriel's nod in her direction was subtle, but she caught the hint. Nose wrinkling—fastidious even in death—Lydia stepped into the cabin on noiseless feet.

"I need to talk to you." For the first time in the short while Adriel had known her, Lydia appeared at a disadvantage. "And I realize I was not at my best the last time we spoke."

Head tilted, Adriel shrugged, but met Lydia's steady gaze. "Then again," she continued with a pointed look, "I had no idea you were an angel."

"That's a subject of great debate at the moment." Adriel said wryly, and twitched her shoulders. Her missing wings sent up phantom tingles every so often.

Lydia glanced around at the dwindling pile of boxes, the shabby but clean kitchen area, and wrinkled her nose again. "This place is a bigger dump than I thought. Did you get on the wrong side of God to end up here?"

Apparently, her acid tongue had accompanied her into the afterlife, and being an angel wasn't proof against it. Discussing her own situation with Lydia wouldn't get Adriel any closer to finding out who had killed the woman. "Never mind that, did you see who hit you?"

A series of emotions chased across Lydia's face until her forehead settled into frown lines, and with a twist of her lips, she said, "I'm afraid I'm not going to be much help. The last thing I remember before waking up dead was leaving my house to go for a walk."

"You must have some idea who had the most motive to hurt you."

"Half the town would be on that list."

This was not news to Adriel, who had yet to run into anyone—other than Lydia's own husband—who genuinely liked the woman.

"What happens next?" Lydia braced herself for the answer, "Shouldn't there have been a light, or a tunnel, or something?"

"You didn't see either of those things before? Do you see them now?" Once, she would have been able to see Lydia's chosen path to the other side; but now, Adriel had to rely on her own perceptions. Lydia looked left, then right. A shiver ran through the earthbound angel when she saw the reflection of the rainbow bridge in the ghost's eyes. It was like getting a tiny glimpse of home.

"I see something. It's calling me. Am I supposed to just go?"

"Do you trust me to find justice for you?"

Lydia eyed Adriel speculatively. What she saw must have been enough to satisfy her. "Yes, I believe you won't rest until you've uncovered the truth."

"Then go." How unfair was it that Lydia could go home, while all Adriel could do was stand here and watch her walk away, fading as she went. At the last second, Lydia turned back.

"For what it's worth, I'm sorry about the way I treated people. There's no excuse for the way I acted. Try not to think badly of me. I really did mean well in my own misguided way." When the last tiny shred of her essence left this plane, it was with a flash of light that widened for a fraction of a second, then flared out.

Zack picked that moment to knock on the frame of Adriel's open door and poke his head inside. When he got a look at the organized chaos in which she lived, his eyes widened and he gave a low whistle. "That's a lot of stuff." It was a vast understatement.

"Really? I hadn't noticed." Adriel's arch tone triggered a quirked smile. She waved a hand to indicate he should join her. "Can I get you anything?" By now, Adriel had watched several episodes of Big Bang Theory—enough to know social convention required her to offer Zack a beverage.

"No, thanks. I'm just here to follow up on your statement. I know it's probably dumb to ask, but is there anything else you remember about finding Lydia? Anything to add to what you've told me already?"

Adriel met his gaze steadily, "No, nothing, but you should know Lydia came by here for a visit. Just now." Given Zack's connections to the other side, he picked up on the implications immediately.

"What is this—Grand Central Spook Station?"

"Just a quick stopover on her way across the bridge to tell me she didn't get a look at her attacker."

"What about last night. Did you hear or see anything?"

A slow shake of her head was his answer.

Zack heaved a sigh. "Looks like I'm going to be out this way a lot over the next few weeks."

"Will you bring Kat?"

"She wants to come. They all do. I told them I thought you needed more time. If you're ready to see them, all I have to do is say the word and they'll invade."

Was she? Running away hadn't been her finest hour, and she was sure they would ask questions she couldn't answer about where she'd been all those months.

Adriel's relationship with the group of women and men who had figured highly during her best—and worst—hour had passed beyond the boundaries of charge and guardian to something more intimate. Not quite friendship, because her job required her to remain impartial, and yet, circumstances had forced something more open, more reciprocal. Each and every one of them had gone to extraordinary lengths to banish an Earthwalker from a man who had hurt each one of them with his actions, and then to save one of their own. If nothing else, she at least owed them a conversation. Surely nothing they could say would make her feel worse about what happened than she already did.

"Yes, please tell them to come."

***

Three days of hard slog cleared the stack of boxes from the porch and reduced the volume in the living room by well over half. Adriel finally felt like she was making progress when the blare of a car horn sounded outside. True to his prediction, Kat sat in the driver's seat of a shiny little compact car. Adriel couldn't have said what make; she preferred older cars to newer ones. To her eye those all looked too much alike. Julie, Gustavia, and Amethyst were crammed in like clowns in a circus car. Gustavia's brightly colored clothing did nothing to dispel the illusion.

Chattering lightheartedly, the four women walked toward the cabin, eyes assessing, yet not judging. Adriel felt a weight lift just knowing they were there. Gustavia, wearing one of her more subdued outfits—a three tiered skirt in pink, green and yellow under a neon green tank, and only two strings of beads—bounced onto the porch to rap on the door.

A flock of butterflies circled Adriel's stomach. Some advance notice would have been nice. Not that she could have tidied up the place in its current condition.

"Galmadriel, are you in there?"

Almost wiping out trying to hurdle a box, Adriel pulled open the door. Hello died on her lips when Gustavia pulled her into a fierce hug before she had the chance to speak. Adriel leaned in, enjoying the sensation, and held on tight. Once Gustavia let her go, the others each took a turn. It had been a mistake to downplay the history they all shared. A bigger one to overlook the value of loving friendships.

These strong, brave women had put themselves firmly in the path of evil in order to protect a man who, frankly, didn't deserve their compassion. Julie's weak-hearted ex-fiancé, Logan Ellis had caused all manner of trouble. First as a con man who tried to bilk Julie out of her property, and then, by becoming the perfect vessel for an ancestor who just happened to be an Earthwalker—a spirit who deliberately refused to cross over for nefarious reasons. It was a choice of dark over light; evil over good. Only the most powerful managed to take over a human vessel the way Billy had with Logan. Moreover, no banished Earthwalker ever left their host alive. Using the unique talents of these four women and their menfolk, Adriel had pulled off the impossible.

"I..." Words failed her. They might not realize how badly wrong things had gone. Now she would have to expose her every mistake.

"Zack told us everything. There's no need to explain it all again." Kat spoke for the group. "Can you ever forgive us for letting you down?"

Adriel searched Kat's face for any sign of the crippling fear her psychic abilities had once produced. Compassionate blue eyes twinkled from under a dark fringe of bangs with no trace of accusation or recrimination. Part of the burden lifted from Adriel's shoulders.

"But it's you who should forgive me. I made a horrible mistake and nearly cost you your life. What happened to me is nothing more than what I deserved."

"Well that's the biggest load of hooey I've ever heard." Amethyst's statement was one of fact, at least as she saw it. Turning to look at her, Adriel found the petite, lavender-haired woman treating her to the same deeply assessing look.

"Your aura has totally changed," she said, her voice deeper than expected from someone who barely topped five feet in height. "It's fascinating." She tilted her head, let her eyes go soft and unfocused, then reached out to pluck at strands of color and light only she could see. "Sorry," she muttered, "I should have asked first. It's just...I'm seeing something...and there it is." A flick of the wrist preceded a smoothing motion. "There's a block, but it's one I can't move. I cleared the way for when you feel ready."

"You seem to have settled in with your new level of aura vision." Amethyst's power tingled along Adriel's skin even though the other woman had not laid so much as finger anywhere on her body. For the first time since waking up human, Adriel felt balanced.

"Remind me to tell you about it sometime." Dry and low, Amethyst's voice rasped. "Today, though, we want to hear about you."

"Here, let me move some things around so we can all sit down. I'll tell you what I know, which isn't really all that much, and then I want to hear about what's been happening to all of you."

"I'll help." Gustavia picked up a plastic bin and shook it to try and guess the contents before moving it out of the way.

Kat gave her an indulgent smile before focusing her attention on Adriel, who rushed to speak.

"Kat, I'm..." Kat held up a hand before Adriel could finish.

"Don't you dare say you're sorry. You helped Zack save me, it's everything." A tear welled at the corner of her eye.

94

"How can you say that? I'm the one who put you in danger to begin with." Twinges of guilt crept back to tweak Adriel's shoulder muscles into tense ropes. Out of the corner of her eye, she saw Amethyst's fingers twitch with the desire to pluck away the pain.

Kat's eyes fired. "No. You. Did. Not." She emphasized each word. "I went into it—we all," she gestured to include her friends, "went into it knowing there was danger. You never forced me to do anything I didn't choose to do."

"Besides, you're looking at it all wrong. We battled the forces of evil. Kat and Amethyst leveled up with their abilities. Jules saved her house, and I got to meet an honest-to-God angel. We kicked Earthwalker butt. We were kind of hoping we could do it again sometime." Gustavia, as usual, cut right to the heart of the matter with precision.

Adriel's mouth dropped open, but nothing came out. She'd been rendered speechless.

"You can't...but I...I thought you'd hate me for what happened."

Amethyst's deep voice enhanced the dry dust of her tone, "You underestimated us. Again."

Adriel couldn't think of anything to say.

Julie, quiet until now, changed the subject. Adriel looked like she needed a few moments to recover her composure. Besides, sheer curiosity forced her to ask, "Cute cabin. What's with the storage unit decor?"

It was a whole other story to tell, and by the time Adriel was finished, Gustavia had a manic gleam in her eye. "You have to let us help. I bet if the five of us worked together, we could clear a bunch of this in a day."

Half of Adriel wanted to say no, it would be too big an imposition—the other half wanted to leap with joy over the prospect of navigating more freely through the small space.

In the end, nothing she said would have mattered anyway; Gustavia would not be contained, they had decided to help, and that was all there was to it.

"It's like Christmas," Gustavia popped the top on an appropriately red plastic bin with a green lid.

Adriel shot her a raised eyebrow and a wry comment, "Twisted Christmas. One man's trash is—well—this mess actually. Knock yourself out."

Amethyst gave Adriel a look somewhere on the spectrum between amused and surprised, "You've loosened up since we saw you last."

"I'm embracing my inner mortal." The grin wouldn't stay off Adriel's face.

"You know you could have just stayed at Hayward House. For as long as you needed." Julie wasn't smiling. "There was no reason you should end up here." She waved a hand to indicate the piles of boxes.

Meeting her eyes tested Adriel's will. "When I woke up and saw the aftermath, I felt so…" words failed her so she flipped a hand in circles, "And then I realized I was human, and I needed time to adjust to my new status. There's work I'm meant to do here. Or so I've been told." Estelle, Adriel's guardian angel, had been Julie's grandmother in life. Mentioning her name right now felt wrong for some reason, so Adriel didn't.

"Ooh, look." Gustavia pulled out a purple metal box decorated with five floating faces on the side. "It's an Osmond Brother's lunch box. From the 1970s."

"Osmond brothers? Weren't they…"

"A singing family. This is a collector's item. I bet it's worth at least fifty dollars."

"That thing? With the disembodied heads? Someone would pay money for that?"

"Yeah, if it has the thermos. Does it have the thermos?" Amethyst arched her back to get a better look.

Gustavia flipped two metal clasps near the handle and the box lid popped open to reveal a tube-like container. She held it aloft, "Yes it does."

"What else is in there?" Amethyst had bin fever now as well. She made Kat budge over so she could sit next to

Gustavia, who now wore a dusty old cloche hat. Spoils from the bin.

"Kat, toss me your keys, I'll go down to the village and grab some pizza or something. We might as well make a party out of it," Julie said. "There's a pizza place, right?" Adriel nodded.

"You did hear me say I'd found boxes of dirty socks, right?" she said to no one, because that's who listened.

Laughter and the smell of pizza soon filled the small space. Kat took the prize for weirdest find of the day—a shoe box full of used coffee filters pressed flat and labeled with images supposedly found in the patterns made by the grounds. No one, not even Gustavia, could make out either Jesus or Elvis in their respective filters.

They filled four totes with items for Hamlin to take to the shelter, topped off the small dumpster for the third or fourth time—Adriel had lost track—and cleared all but half a dozen of the remaining boxes in less time than it would have taken Adriel to move a single stack by herself.

Gustavia went home with the cloche hat and, because it was purple, Amethyst took the floating head lunch box. More important than what they took home, though, was what they left behind: phone numbers on the refrigerator and an Adriel with a much lighter heart.

***

"That went well, don't you think?" Gustavia chirped as Kat reversed out of the drive. "I was afraid she might be all depressed over not being an angel anymore."

"About that," Amethyst said, "I assume she knows, but she's no human. Or not entirely anyway. Her aura is a mess. I mean, I sorted out what I could, but it's still the strangest blend I've ever seen. There are angel winding around the human, and the block I told you about is just crazy big. I'm

97

not even sure the angel side of her is strong enough to move it alone. What did you think, Kat?"

"Oh, I agree with you. I sensed both angel and human. But what really had me worried was seeing she's touched something dark lately as well. Zack was right to send us. There's trouble coming, and she's going to need help."

The grin slid off Gustavia's face to be replaced with a look of determination. "Whether she wants it or not, right?"

"Did you notice she never mentioned Grams or Julius?" As much concern as she had for Adriel, Julie wanted to know the fate of her family members, too. "I'd feel better if she could tell me they made it out okay. I know we agreed before we came if it looked like she needed more time, we would keep things light, but let's make sure she doesn't retreat back into whatever shell she stayed in for three months."

Gustavia pulled the cloche from her head to twist it in her hands. "The way she talked, it was as though she'd gone straight from Hayward House to Longbrook. No mention of those three months at all. We needed another mystery to solve, it's been way too quiet lately."

Chapter Nine

True to her word, Pam showed up two days a week to help with cleaning and trash removal. After Adriel's productive day with the gang from Oakville, Pam's arrival on a rainy Friday morning was the first where there was little left to do.

"I've got some errands to do in Bridgeport today. You want to come along? You can meet Uncle Craig—see the face behind the mess." A wistful hope flitted across Pam's features and the words *so lonely* popped into Adriel's head. Curiosity about the man who spent what must have been a considerable part of his life boxing up random items was secondary to spending time with Pam, who seemed to need a friend.

Gray drizzle fell from a gray sky, leaving Adriel feeling slightly blue. Why not spend a day somewhere besides these four walls?

"Sure."

Had she remembered Pam's complete abandon behind the wheel of her Jeep, Adriel might have given a smidge more thought to the decision. Good thing there was a handle just above the passenger side door. Adriel clung to it like a leech while Pam, talking a blue streak the entire time, sent the vehicle careening around corners and rocketing along straightaways way too fast for the wet road conditions. It felt like she probably shaved three minutes off the time it would have taken a normal driver to get there—and maybe a few years off Adriel's life as well.

They pulled to an abrupt, Jeep-rocking halt mere fractions of an inch from the curb in front of a rambling, single-floored brick building. Amaretti Senior Housing boasted a nearly full residency section and updated facilities to provide long or short-term care. Cheerful flowers provided lovely, if slightly soggy color along the path to the door, and Adriel noted a sizable fenced-in area planted liberally with vegetables.

As the two women made ready to enter the building, a man who appeared spry for his age bolted through the doors shouting for someone named Brenda. An energetic orderly with an umbrella shot past to collar and then gently coax the elderly man back inside. On his way past, he gave an apologetic glance. "Mr. Mason gets a little anxious sometimes."

Pam waved to the woman behind the reception desk on the way through, and led Adriel down a carpeted corridor to the left, where she knocked on the third from the last right-hand door. The sound of someone mumbling could be heard through the wooden panel before Pam turned the knob and Adriel followed her into the room.

Uncle Craig's room was in the early stages of taking up where his cabin had left off. Several stacks of bins stood along one wall—filled with whatever detritus he'd managed to collect. Adriel was glad it was never going to be her job to find out.

Younger than Adriel expected, Craig appeared to be no older than sixty. Not quite frail, yet no longer the robust man he had clearly once been, Craig's stooped shoulders straightened when he saw Pam.

Standing in the center of the room, he had been carrying on a conversation with young Ben, who glanced at the newcomers and winked out of sight. Seeing the two of them together raised questions Adriel knew she could not ask in front of Pam. Toddlers, the elderly, and the mentally infirm were often among those able to see and speak to lingering spirits, because their vibrational energies were closer to those on the other side.

100

"Uncle Craig, I've brought someone to meet you," she gestured vaguely behind her. "This is Adriel." Now came the moment of truth. If Craig could see Ben, he might also be able to parse Adriel's dual nature and reveal her secret. The tilt of his head and the squint in his eye did not bode well. Standing firm under his gaze, Adriel felt as though he looked right through her to the truth of her being. It was a most uncomfortable experience. For a moment, his vision seemed clearer, saner than it had when they walked in. He reached out to place a hand on her shoulder and nodded his head before his eyes returned to a less-than-focused state.

A string of nonsense words flowed past his lips.

"Looks like one of his bad days," Pam said. "We won't stay long." She bustled around the room watering a flourishing philodendron and pulling several drooping, brown-edged carnations from the colorful bouquet of flowers in a cut glass vase near the bed. Next, Pam opened the drawer to drop several candy bars into the nightstand and, turning to Adriel, said, "I like to make sure he has his chocolate. On the worst weeks he forgets to eat them, so it gives me a good idea of how he's been when I check his stash." To Craig, she kept up a running commentary on news from home. None of it registered with him.

"Look." Adriel nearly leapt out of her skin at the touch of Estelle's hand on her shoulder. The new angel sent out tendrils of energy, pulled Adriel along to take a short peek into his mind. What she saw surprised her. Echoing the cabin and his room here, she found herself in a maze of compartmentalized thoughts and emotions. Only this was on an epic scale. Alleys leading to dead ends, circular paths leading nowhere, and so many twists and turns it would be nearly impossible to find the way back to a particular area of his memory. In horror Adriel realized he was lost and captive within the vast maze of his own life experiences. Given time and the return of her abilities, she thought she might be able to help him create anchors and decrease the amount of time he spent wandering aimlessly. For the moment, all she could do was call him toward one of the sections closest to the present.

Detaching from his mind when Estelle withdrew her energy, Adriel saw his eyes were now more focused. He turned them on Pam with a warm smile that she returned.

"Uncle Craig, it's me, Pam."

"Well, of course I know that. See you with my own eyes, don't I?" There was no rebuke to his tone. He glanced around the room as though unsure, for a moment, where he was. Clicked in for the time being, Adriel saw him recognize his surroundings, noticed the quickly-covered dismay on his face. "Gone again, wasn't I?"

"Yes. You were." Pam laid a hand on his arm. "But you're back now."

Craig's U-shaped room was about the size of the cabin the illness forced him to leave behind. The bathroom took up most of the central portion of the U, and provided some privacy to the two sleeping areas flanked on either side. At the lower end of the U, Craig and his currently-absent roommate shared a communal sitting area containing two vinyl-covered sofas with a small table between them. Every piece of furniture was bolted to the floor. Once Pam got the three of them seated on the sofas, she launched again into the pertinent news from home until he interrupted her with a comment that made Adriel's blood run cold. "You find your brother yet? He was here a little while ago."

She needn't have worried, Pam brushed off the honest truth because it was too fantastic for her to consider. "No, Ben hasn't come home." She busied herself again by checking through more of his things to make sure he had what he needed until her next visit. Adriel wanted to ask how often Ben stopped by, and had the pair of them been in contact all along, or was it a recent development. One look at Pam's stiff spine and the way her hands jerked with every motion was enough to deter the conversation.

Instead, the next few seconds were spent having a private inner war with herself over begging Estelle to help her rove a little deeper through Craig's mind. If her powers had remained intact, Adriel would have interfered enough to place a few markers he could follow back to the present. Her intuition insisted there was enough vital information stored in the chaos of his mind to make it worth meddling, even if doing so was frowned upon by those in charge of these types of things.

Temptation won out. While Pam indulged in delighted conversation with Craig, Adriel silently argued her case with Estelle. A few harmless signposts for him to follow wouldn't be enough to keep him fully anchored, but should decrease the amount of time lost to the vagaries of his memory. When gentle persuasion looked like it wasn't working, Adriel put her foot down.

"I'm in charge of your training, right? Then consider this a lesson in how to heal. It's a skill you might be called upon to use. Besides, a saner Craig might be able to help Ben, while giving Pam a little more peace of mind."

Mentally thumbing her nose at the powers that be, Adriel borrowed on Estelle's power to start placing signposts throughout Craig's mind.

Each new marker led her farther into the maze, until a turn separated her from Estelle and in her haste to get back, she went one section too far. Then another and another, until she realized she was getting close to the center of the maze where something lurked. A presence trying hard to present itself as null, but had the flavor and scent of malevolence. Angel power flared through her like a sleek, black panther uncurling to stalk prey. Adriel nearly cried at the familiarity of feeling totally connected to her truth again.

The sense of rightness faded when a furious Estelle rounded the corner. "What are you doing? You said a couple markers around the edges and the next thing I know, you're gone."

Whatever rested in Craig's mind would have to wait— Estelle was done with rule breaking.

Estelle, dragging Adriel along behind her, pulled back to the edge of Craig's mind as quickly as she could without hurting him. To her surprise, Craig's spirit was there to meet them.

"You're going to help the boy." He made it a statement instead of a question.

"That is the plan," Adriel answered. "Can you tell me anything helpful?" Craig turned his back on them; Adriel and Estelle exchanged a glance. He did know something.

"Just help him. He's the key to it all. The lies, and the secrets, and the shame." Craig was getting worked up. Adriel needed to do something to calm him before Pam noticed anything funny going on.

"Trust me." An unexpected flare of her old authority—born of speaking only truth—bolstered the words into an intonation that made him flinch as it echoed through his head. She felt bad about basically yelling at the poor man. Then he nodded his head and relaxed with a small smile. Back in her own mind, Adriel saw Pam preparing to leave.

"I'm so sorry," she said once we were back in the Jeep. "I've never seen him get worked up like that before. He's usually pretty docile."

Was there anything Adriel could tell Pam to ease her mind? The debate raged through her while Pam took her lack of response for something other than an innocent pause. When Adriel realized her hesitation was adding to Pam's general sense of unease, she said "He seemed to be more lucid when we left."

"When he said he'd seen Ben, it sent a chill up my spine. For all I know, it could be true. He could be alive and living nearby, and I'd have spent my life waiting for a reunion that would never come. Why would he do that and never contact me?"

Knowing she needed to pick her words carefully, Adriel said, "What do you think happened to him?"

A moment slid by while Pam framed her answer. "Kids end up on milk cartons all the time. He could have run away; he could have been abducted." Her voice dropped an octave, quavered slightly, "He could be dead. They're all horrible options. I can't believe he would leave us voluntarily."

"So you've ruled out him becoming a runaway."

"My parents were older than most when they started their family. Daddy died on the operating table ten years after we lost Ben. Complications from a minor surgery. Mother left the porch light on for the rest of her life. Every night for twenty-six years. A shining beacon to guide Ben if he ever came home. She never stopped hoping. When she passed, I had a choice—keep the house and leave the light burning, or sell the place and accept my brother was gone. I sold the house. What does that tell you?"

"It must have been a difficult decision."

"If he could have come home, he would have done it a long time ago."

"So you think he's…"

"Dead. I think he's dead." A pause. "I've never said it out loud. I was always afraid saying it would make it true. And yet, I've stayed in this hole of a town, waiting. Just in case." Bitterness twisted her lips. "Maybe Mother wasn't the only one with delusions."

"I'm sorry." Adriel's heart broke for Pam. Not knowing Ben's fate had taken a toll on her. Telling Pam what she knew might help the woman make sense of her loss, or it might make things worse. Without evidence, all Adriel could give her was a fantastic story and more speculation.

Outside the Jeep, everything stopped. Even Pam froze in time. Estelle had returned.

"Nice trick. You're learning."

From the back seat, Estelle said, "You can't tell her yet."

"I know." Pique at being second-guessed wove through Adriel's tone. Left alone, she might have tried to clue Pam in, though.

"Don't get crabby with me; I'm just the messenger."

"Not my first day." Feeling defensive was a new emotion—one Adriel could have lived without.

"You talked me into meddling in the man's mind," Estelle's words were an accusation. "And you knew it was against the rules."

"Only a little."

Estelle's skeptical squint said more than words. "If he was supposed to be healed in this manner, his guardian would already have done so."

"Not necessarily. A guardian should respect whatever choice a charge makes when it comes to issues like this. As long as it doesn't interfere with the growth or safety of another. When there are additional factors like there are with this case—Pam, Ben, what happened with Lydia—a different course of action may be needed. He knows something, and without intervention the information might be lost. Plus, I couldn't stand to see either of them in so much pain. Giving him a bit more lucidity seemed like a good compromise. What could it hurt?"

"I'm new to this angel stuff, but even I know that's a bit of human justification. How are you supposed to train me properly if you can't stay detached?"

Estelle's disappointment left Adriel feeling like a chastised child. "I'm sorry. These human emotions are irrational sometimes, and a lot stronger than I ever expected. How people manage to hold up under the stress is beyond me. I feel like I'm being pulled in different directions all the time." Estelle's eyes flitted upward as she processed this information. When speculation narrowed them slightly, Adriel found herself becoming angry. "Don't look at me like that. You should know what I'm talking about, you were human not so long ago yourself. None of this is new to you. Me? I've always been an angel until now. I'm not some test subject or one of those rodent whatsits," Adriel snapped her fingers while she pulled the word from her mind, "wait, I remember. I'm not a Guinea Pig."

"Technically, you are, though." Estelle disagreed gently.

"Oink." Adriel wrinkled her nose.

"Guinea Pigs don't oink. They whistle."

"Is that really germane to the conversation?"

Humor twitched Estelle's mouth into a smile holding a level of fondness most angels learned to control in the early days of working with humans. As part of her training, Adriel should be telling Estelle it was time to become more detached, but lacking any other allies at the moment she chose to remain silent.

"Probably not."

"I'm working on gut instinct most of the time. Sometimes human, sometimes angel. Make no mistake, you and Julius are in this as deeply as I am. If I'm a whistle pig, you're another." Estelle's shoulders twitched and the smile never left her face. She was enjoying this too much, in Adriel's opinion. "Craig's mind looks a lot like his house—full of walls and maze paths. I suspect he's trying to bury his memories and ,following that logic, there's info stored in there somewhere I think will help me figure out how Ben died. With him going in and out of lucidity, the only way to get at what he knows is to go in there myself. I thought it better to help him think more clearly so he can make a choice."

Compassion for humans was stock in trade for angels. Compassion tempered with a certain level of detachment—so when a charge needed to go through something painful in order to learn a lesson, the guardian knew when not to step in and take away the pain. That sense of detachment didn't stand up to human hormones, and Adriel had those in spades.

"Be careful," Estelle warned. "You'll still have to answer for your actions."

"This one's not on me. There's something else taking up space in his head. Something that feels evil."

"Earthwalker?"

"Not sure. We'll need to take a closer look."

As Adriel watched, Estelle's eyes turned unfocused. She was listening to a command from home.

"I have to go. I'll be in touch." Time snapped back into forward motion leaving Adriel with several thoughts chasing around her head.

***

"You need a cell phone," Pam declared with finality.

"I'm sure I don't."

"Trust me, you do. We'll go get you one of those prepaid ones. That way, you won't have a monthly bill to worry about, but you'll have it in case of emergencies. It's your first big step toward being more independent. First a phone, then a car." Pam dragged Adriel past shelves piled high with various gadgets and over to the mobile phone department. Given her history with all things electrical, there was a better than even chance she would kill a cell phone inside of a week.

"I don't drive." Pam gave Adriel that look. The one combining sympathy with the words, what planet are you from? Adriel hated that look but couldn't disagree with the sentiment behind it—from Pam's perspective, she was as odd as they come.

"I'll teach you."

"I don't need you to embark on a program for my betterment."

"Nonsense. Everyone should learn to drive. It's a rite of passage."

"I didn't say I couldn't drive. I said I don't. There's a difference." Adriel's tone of absolute finality deterred Pam about as much as a bird could stop a hurricane, and earned her the look a second time. In return, Adriel blasted Pam with her patented I'm-an-angel-don't-mess-with-me glare, which only proved Pam was impervious. Adriel might as well have handed her a kitten for all the good it did.

"What did you do to get from place to place? Teleport?" The joke fell on stony ground since it was a bit too close to the truth for Adriel's comfort. Pam's eyes lit with the fervor normally reserved for religious zealots when she picked out the phone she thought would suit Adriel best.

108

"Here; this one can access the Internet and take photos." Clutching a blister-wrapped packaged, she then dragged Adriel to the checkout.

Back in the parking lot, Pam's flashing legs carried her straight to the passenger seat. The little woman could move fast when she wanted to. Smirking smugly, she chirped, "You drive."

"I don't drive." Insistence appeared futile.

"Whatever it is, you need to get over it. It's four miles. What harm could you do in so short of a distance. Besides, you did say you knew how. Prove it."

"It would be illegal."

"Come on, take a walk on the wild side."

"Don't say I didn't warn you." Adriel twisted the key and the motor hummed to life. With shaking hands, she dropped the shifter into reverse, looked over her shoulder, and stepped on the gas. The Jeep shot out of the space like a rocket, and if her reflexes hadn't been sharp, would have slammed into one of the cars parked in the next row. Jamming the brake, Adriel managed to stop just in the nick of time, while Pam rocked forward then backward in her seat—one hand gripping the seatbelt, the other braced on the dash.

Nervous energy lifted the hair on Adriel's arms to the point of creating a prickling sensation. Absently, Pam let go of the seat belt to brush a hand down her own arm—so strong was the wave of energy pouring through the small space.

Shifting into drive, Adriel attempted to take off at a slower pace. She really did. What felt to her like gentle pressure on the pedal caused the vehicle to lurch forward. Heightened emotion pushed at the boundary of the block around her power until more of it leaked into the frisson of tension running along her skin. Pam's GPS crackled to life without being turned on and announced, *you have arrived* before going dead. Presumably forever.

"But I've barely even left yet."

Pam's laugh was half amused and half horrified. Goosebumps flowed across her skin like a wave. Any sane person would have demanded to take over the wheel. Instead, she waved Adriel on like an adrenaline junkie getting a fix. Tossing her head back and laughing harder had the opposite effect of calming Adriel down. The more Pam seemed to enjoy the ride, the harder the experience played on Ariel's nerves, and the more intense the waves of energy radiated off her. Pam should have been begging to stop by now, instead of laughing like an overjoyed hyena.

This wasn't Adriel's first time behind the wheel of a vehicle. She hadn't lied about that; but would Pam believe her if she explained the last time was when she filled in for a NASCAR driver's guardian angel? The time before that was during a short stint with Henry Ford. A car is a car, right?

By the time they pulled into Adriel's drive, Pam had finally gone quiet. And pale. And she was sweating from places Adriel didn't even know had sweat glands.

"You know what?" Pam choked out the words, "I think Uncle Craig had a bike in the shed. Maybe you should check it out. I think it had a nice basket on the front." Her voice trembled, "They say exercise does a body good."

***

Over Pam's shoulder, Julius shimmered into view. "Come outside," he mouthed. Adriel gave him a nearly imperceptible nod and excused herself. Her shift wouldn't start until after noon, so she said goodbye to Pam and strolled out of the building.

"Hello, Julius. Good to see you again."

His head bobbed. "Galmadriel." He fell silent.

"I assume you're here in the same capacity as Estelle?" Wry humor penetrated her tone. In her present predicament, training the pair of them wouldn't be easy, and she suspected they might have been sent to her as penance. She strolled with him toward home.

"We let you down at the bridge. I'm sorry."

"I'm the one who let you down. I should have known it would be too much for us to handle."

Adriel chanced a glance at him to find his face unreadable. Taciturn at the best of times, Julius kept his feelings locked down tightly. It was a habit that would stand him in good stead as a guardian. Most of the time, anyway. His head bobbed again and then he turned a wide grin her way.

"You sure turned some heads with that stunt. Half the collective is annoyed you got away with it. The other half are impressed you had the strength to pull it off, and they're all trying to figure out how to capitalize on your new status. What with everything that's happened since..."

This was news to Adriel. Estelle only provided limited details.

"Everything that's happened since? Do you know what they're going to do with me?" The minute the words came out, Adriel wished she hadn't asked. His expression turned guarded and he kicked a small, round stone hard enough for it to go skittering down the road ahead of them. When he didn't answer, she pressed, "Can you at least tell me what happened during those three months I was missing?" Julius' mouth pressed itself into a straight line. Whatever he knew, he wasn't talking. "Then what are you doing here?" Frustration ebbed out with the question.

"On the job training, which means you're supposed to tell me what to do next."

Unexpected angry heat burned across Adriel's skin, reddened her face. Yelling at Julius, while satisfying, wouldn't address the root of her concerns. "You see how this is a problem, right?"

"I see how you're supposed to tell me what to do next."

Him repeating it wasn't going to solve anything.

"I don't have enough information."

Julius sighed impatiently. "You're my teacher, so *tell me what you want me to do*." His exaggerated emphasis finally penetrated Adriel's thick skull.

"Oh." Her eyes widened.

"Well then, Julius, you need to tell me everything you know about my current assignment." He raised an eyebrow and circled his hand to indicate she needed to say more. "And anything about my last one you think might be helpful to my ability to complete it."

Relief sagged his shoulders. "Since you've given me a direct order, here's what I can tell you..." A thunderclap shook the air, made the earth tremble under their feet. With no other warning, Julius disappeared. So much for getting any useful information out of him.

The next thing Adriel felt was an icy cold hand gripping her arm. Night-black darkness descended over her like a cloud bringing with it an unearthly silence. She yanked her arm away hard, but the hand grasping it only tightened painfully. Red eyes gleamed a feral warning when she turned her head toward the source of pain. Vertigo threatened to suck Adriel toward an abyss just out of her line of sight. Her heart galloped into a staccato beat that her ears seemed to feel, rather than hear. Goosebumps pebbled every inch of exposed skin.

A low hissing broke through the sound of her blood rushing through her veins "You took one of mine, I'll take one of yours." Breath reeking of death and oozing decay overwhelmed her senses. Out of the hulking darkness, the likeness of the Earthwalker she had recently banished swam toward her, pure terror contorting his face into a silent scream. "Or I will take everything." Image after image of her friends shrieking in agony swam out of the darkness, then faded back into oblivion. Her ears popped and their screams turned audible. Slamming her hands over her ears did nothing to mute the sounds. Even her own voice raised to its highest pitch couldn't wash away their tormented cries.

When the darkness finally faded, Adriel found herself huddled in a ball at the end of the cabin's short driveway; Julius nowhere in sight. Chest still heaving, ears ringing with the sound of her own screams, she made her way to the bathroom and stripped to stand under the steaming spray. Heat

112

returned to chilled limbs slowly, but nothing could wash away the sights and sounds of her friends being dragged into the dark realm while she watched in paralyzed horror.

Too rattled to settle, she paced the twisted path between the boxes from one end of the tiny space to the other—over and over until it felt like her feet might sink into the worn floorboards. Each time she walked past it the phone caught her eye. A magnet pinned Kat's number to the refrigerator. All she needed to do was pick up the phone, punch the buttons and in no time, the cabin would be filled with the very faces playing through her mind right now.

"Julius!" She called his name loudly. "Estelle. I need you!" As though an invisible dome arched over her head, each cry bounced and echoed back to her—the words falling like stones around her head.

Despair licked at the edge of her thoughts until fury pushed it back. No more. Instead of banking the fire, she let the anger burn higher, brighter, stronger. What erupted from her was more than a request, it was an order backed by every ounce of rage-fueled angel power she had ever had at her disposal. The force of it blew the hair back from her face.

"Come to me, now!"

The form shimmering before her turned out not to be Estelle or Julius. Nope. That would have been too easy.

"You wanted something?" Chiseled features; skin brushed with every shade of gold; pale blue eyes glowing with crystal fire: Malachiel stood in the tiny room. His wings brushed the ceiling, their tips dragged on the floor. No angel ever looked so uncomfortable.

"Don't bother giving me your patented how-dare-you stare. After what happened earlier, it's somewhere around the third scariest thing I've seen today. Put your wings away and sit down. It's about time I got some answers." Watching him try to navigate the room while stubbornly keeping his wings in corporeal form brought a tiny smile.

"Tell me what happened during the time I lost." She watched his face carefully for anything useful.

113

"What do you remember?" His eyes flickered.

"I remember every second of eternity except for the time between when I left Hayward House and ended up here. Now tell me what happened during those months."

"I cannot." At least he was being honest this time.

"What can you tell me?"

"Nothing. No one is going to tell you anything."

"Why did you bother to come here, then?"

"Your anger called me. You'd better watch out, Galmadriel. How far do you really want to fall?" Was that a warning? Adriel wasn't sure.

"At least tell me what you know about Julius."

At Malachiel's blank look, Adriel said, "Here's what happened." She laid out the events of the past hour for him in fine detail. If he knew anything about the entity that had accosted her, his carefully schooled features gave away nothing.

Chapter Ten

One more day, Gideon promised. One more day, and his crew would lay a culvert to connect this trench with the one on the other side of the road. To get the job done faster, he brought in two of the scooping machines from hell. One to hack out the section of road where the pipe would go, the other to finish the last bit of the trench leading up to it. What Gideon failed to mention was the need for tamping soil down tightly over the corrugated length of pipe. Added to the constant digging noises was the sound of the second bucket pounding soil into place.

Bang. Bang. Bang.

Adriel went about her business for the morning praying for a freak accident to render her temporarily deaf. Not that it would have mattered, given the shock waves accompanying the banging sound could be felt through the floor.

When the pounding stopped, shouting replaced the short reprieve of silence.

Not the kind of shouting of orders being given or taken, though. This shouting sounded altogether different. She stopped to listen.

"...there's the skull, and that's a hand."

Skull? An ominous sounding word. Ominous enough to make her open the door and go see what was happening.

An interesting tableau spread itself before Adriel when she stepped onto the porch. Several men stood, slack-jawed, gazing into a newly dug section running alongside the road, while others milled around as far from the area as they could get. Gideon shouted rapidly into his cell phone.

"No....Roman, I've lived here my whole life, there's no abandoned grave yard around here. You'd better come out and take a look."

Adriel heard the familiar sound of Ben's bicycle long before he pulled to a stop next to the hole. He looked down, his eyes dark pools in a grave, white face. Talking to him in front of the crew was not a valid option, so they both only nodded a hello.

The human nature lurking inside her liked the idea of cowering inside while someone else dealt with the situation. She had always thought fear was an emotional response, but it seemed the heebie jeebies might just be hard wired into the physical body. Curiosity, more than anything, was what finally propelled her feet toward the hole.

After a first look, she hoped it was the depth of the hole making the bleached white bones seem so small, but she knew better. Ben had been found. If there were any doubts, the stricken look in his eyes was enough to dispel them. She longed to talk to him, make him feel better any way she could, but with the entire road crew close enough to remain within hearing distance, it was impossible. Okay, not technically impossible, but not the recommended choice.

It's funny how people's reactions are so different. Based on the way Gideon took charge until Zack arrived, it was easy to see how the job had come to him. He barked orders with no visible sentiment other than the faint whiff of annoyance Adriel could sense, because this was going to put him behind again. Yet, the gruff sympathy in his voice matched the way his eyes strayed time and again back to where the pale relic lay alone and bare in its grave.

No flashing lights or sirens marked Zack's approach this time. There was no reason for hurry, the bones had lain in that spot for long years, and another ten minutes wasn't going to change anything. He flashed Adriel a questioning look, which she answered with a small nod, knowing he would find her when he had time to talk. When she looked back, Ben had gone and Pam's Jeep was pulling into her driveway.

Adriel went out to meet her. "They're saying it's Ben." Not a lick of color graced Pam's face. Tiny freckles stood out against the pale.

"I'll walk with you." Adriel linked arms with Pam knowing it would be a waste of time trying to talk her out of looking at what lay in the cold ground.

***

"Can I get you anything? Iced tea? Coffee?" Adriel offered an hour later when Zack tapped on the screen door before letting himself inside. He noted the changes to the place with a look of approval.

"I'm good." Zack remained standing just inside the door; this was official business. A nodding gesture indicated the hole that marred the edge of Adriel's yard. "You get a chance to see what they found?" She joined him just in time to see a black body bag being slid into the back of an ambulance by a somber-faced man she assumed was the coroner, and the same fellow who had worked hard in his attempt to save Lydia's life.

"Bones." An internal debate ran through her head. Should she tell him she was almost certain she know whose bones they had been?"

"A forensic expert is on the way, but I've seen enough death to know those are the bones of a child, and they've been in the ground for a long time. There's only one missing persons case involving a child fitting the time frame."

Before she could stop the name, it crossed her lips, "Ben Allen?"

"How did you know?"

"I work for Ben's sister, Pam." Should she tell him the rest? Yeah, probably. "And, he's been visiting me."

"He's not an Earthwalker?" Zack's horrified expression said he might have nightmares about devil children if she didn't dispel the notion quickly enough.

"No. It was a genuine case of unfinished business. His death might have been accidental, or it might have been homicide. From what he remembers, it's hard to tell. He was the victim of a hit and run—car vs. bike. There's not much more I can tell you because Ben only got a quick glance at the headlights."

"That explains the death, not the disappearance," Zack said.

"I gather the driver panicked and buried Ben's body"

"Poor kid." Zack's voice dropped in sympathy.

"Looks like he is stuck here until his killer is found." Adriel brought Zack up to date on her conversations with Ben, who hadn't given them much to go on.

"Never a dull moment around you, is there?"

"Ah. Do you...have you..." Adriel wasn't exactly sure how to frame the question. "Would it help if I arranged a visit from Ben? I assume you have questions. I could interpret if you need me to. Or Kat could. Unless you can talk to him yourself since your trip over the bridge," she ended lamely.

"No, I wouldn't be able to see or hear him. We've only run into one other death in connection with a case in the past few months. Not a murder, but we did think it was a suicide. Guy's ghost stuck around long enough to describe his freak accident. Forensics confirmed it after Kat's unofficial investigation, and we closed the case." Adriel could hear the pride in his voice.

"You'll need to talk to Pam. Be gentle with her, Zack. She's more fragile than she seems. Ben was here right after they found the bones. If he comes back, is there anything you want me to ask him that I haven't already?"

"Do you think he would be willing to talk to me? Through you, I mean."

"I'll ask, but I think it's safe to say he would. He's ready to move on."

Zack handed her his card. "Call me if and when. Try to make it soon, though." The screen door squeaked on hinges no amount of oil would quiet when Zack swung back through on his way out.

***

With all the lights off in the cabin, the velvet sky filled with winking stars mirrored flashes from lighting bugs flitting their complicated dance in the field. Night birds called out the news of the day to each other from perches high in the trees. From her chair on the porch, Adriel listened to the soft chirp of insects, the rustle of a low breeze through maple leaves, and the whisper of wind as it tickled the grass. The night soothed her into a peaceful stupor until something odd caught her eye. No lightning bug, this. A penlight not quite shielded enough to remain hidden swung in a slow arc—forward then down—as though its holder was looking for something. Curiosity stilled her tongue.

Moving toward the area where she had found Lydia, the light bounced once and Adriel heard a low, muttered curse in a male voice she didn't recognize. "Stupid rock. Never going to find anything in the dark. What was I thinking coming out here this time of night?" An older man by the sound of his voice.

"Can I help you?" She finally spoke into the darkness.

The penlight jerked then aimed right into her eyes. It was brighter than expected, given that the man holding it was at least twenty feet away. She held up a hand to shield the glare, then stepped down from the porch to close the distance between them.

"My name is Adriel." She squinted to try and see his face. He lowered the light.

"Edward Keough," rough with emotion, his voice sounded a little out of breath. "Folks call me Ed. You're the one who found my Lydia. I wasn't expecting to run into you tonight," or anyone else if he had his way about it, she'd

119

wager. "Would you mind telling me about how you found her?"

"Only if you'll come sit on the porch." The last thing she wanted was for him to keel over in her front yard. "Can I get you anything?" She flipped on the porch light before getting him settled on a lime green plastic chair. Craig had a liking for bright colors.

"Wouldn't say no to a glass of iced tea if you have some." Ed flicked off the penlight and Adriel got her first look at him. Grief dimmed, but couldn't hide the smile lines around his mouth and a pair of kindly blue eyes. Age had salted his hair, cut short on both sides, to a crisp white. She judged him as being at least fifteen years older than his late wife. Maybe more.

"I've got lemonade."

"That'll do."

Adriel stepped over the long legs kicked out in front of him to go inside and pour them both a glass. She took her time, giving him a chance to rest and regain his breath. Besides, she wasn't looking forward to this conversation. Telling him the details of finding his wife after her brutal attack didn't rate anywhere on her list of fun things to do.

He took the tall glass of lemonade and drank gratefully.

"I'd like to thank you for what you did for Lydia."

"You're welcome. I'm sorry for your loss."

Ed snorted. "Appreciate that. Lydia wasn't well liked around town. I know that. She knew it, too. She liked things to be just so, and didn't much care whether it was her business to judge others for not feeling the same; but she meant well. In her own way."

While Adriel wondered how he had found the strength to walk here, and whether it would be polite to ask, she let him ramble on about Lydia until he was back on more stable footing.

"Tell me how you found her."

Adriel's brain immediately supplied the truth. She'd been guided to Lydia by the voice of one of her former colleagues.

Estelle refused to admit it straight out, but it wasn't much of a stretch to fill in the blanks. However, blurting out the truth wouldn't be her best choice, and every attempt at prevaricating had failed. She faced a dilemma.

"Destiny." It sounded lame to her, even though the answer had an odd effect on him. Sighing, his shoulders lost the tenseness that had kept them pinched slightly together, and he relaxed. What was that all about? Did he have something to hide?

"She'd only been gone from the house for a short time. You didn't hear anything? See anyone?"

"No. I'm sorry. I told Zack everything. I wish I could be more help." This man, one who by all accounts had been bedridden for months, still managed to make his way here today. Maybe he'd done it before. Not for the first time—or even the hundredth—Adriel wished for her powers back. One quick probe would reveal Edward's every secret.

Not that she would employ that method now. In her time among them, Adriel had begun to learn why every human kept secrets. When your soul is caught between the light and the dark, sometimes the dark wins. Oh, not always in the bigger ways, but those split-second impulses when spite overcomes charitable thought and vitriol spews out on someone who didn't deserve it. Or when temptation pulls and sucks away common sense. Most of those secrets are spawned in arrogance and concealed in shame. Without transgression, there was no way to understand redemption. These lies and regrets were all part of growing.

Adriel suspected Lydia's death was part of Ben's story. What if she'd been wrong all this time, and the two deaths were unrelated? Edward sneaking around after dark and letting people think he was incapacitated was shadier than the dappled light underneath a weeping willow.

"...thought of her lying there alone and in pain, even for a few minutes, is intolerable."

"If it helps, I didn't sense she was in any discomfort."

He wanted to believe. Everything about him reached toward that ideal like a flower trying to touch the sun. "You can't know that."

Actually, she could. But she wasn't about to explain how she came by her information, so she patted his arm in sympathy. Her touch unlocked the floodgates, and he started to talk about his wife. He painted a very different picture from the one Pam had given Adriel.

It hadn't been malice behind Lydia reporting her neighbor for building a temporary lean-to shed to cover his lawn tractor for the winter—the man hadn't hired an architect to design the structure. Surely it would fall on him, and it was Lydia's civic duty to protect the poor wight from his own folly. The eyesore of a boulder in their lower field had nothing to do with her reasons for digging a half mile-long, unnecessary ditch. The new in-ground pool two doors farther up the hill might rupture, and all those gallons of water needed somewhere to go. Why, she was only protecting the town from a deluge. It was nothing more than solid common sense.

Every time Adriel felt an eyebrow raising incredulously, she forced it back down. Even a not-quite human with very little experience in day-to-day living could see through these excuses like they were made of glass. After her death, even Lydia realized it was hogwash. Nevertheless, Adriel let him wind down until he'd talked himself out; plied him with sympathy and two more glasses of lemonade.

"So, you see, she was misunderstood at every turn. My wife was a good woman who only..."

"Shame how they found that boy buried out here, don't you think?" Adriel cut him off mid-sentence with no regret for being rude, then intently watched him form a response. Strong emotion flickered across his face. Not guilt. Guilt was too strong a word. Adriel decided it was remorse. He chose his next words carefully.

"The whole town searched for him for weeks. When nothing turned up, talk turned ugly. People figured he'd run away from home. I never bought that story. The Allens were decent folk. Not the kind a young boy would take to the streets to get away from, you know? But, people talked. Before long, there was speculation about abuse. Funny how people take to whatever suggestion comes up—after a month or so, someone called in the state. Instead of helping with the search, they sent social services."

Someone? *Oh, I wonder who that might have been*, Adriel thought sarcastically. "The results?"

"Nothing. There was nothing to find. The daughter went up one side of the social worker and down the other about how her parents never raised a hand to her or her brother, and how he would never leave his happy family. Fiery little thing. From what I heard, she backed that social worker into a corner."

My heart went out to Pam and her family. First to lose their son so mysteriously, then to be investigated for allegations that cast doubt on the family—whether disproved or not.

"And no one noticed a freshly dug grave when it was right out in plain sight? How could they not?"

"Well, you see, back in those days, there was a stand of pine trees running on the property line between this place and ours. Big bone of contention between Lydia and Craig when she proved they were straddling the line and had them cut down." Judging from his chagrined expression, the trees had probably been Craig's all along. "That must have been six or seven years ago, now," Ed mused.

"So the grave would have been hidden by the lower branches?"

"Must have been hard work digging under there, but easy to conceal. Sweep the downed pine spills out of the way, then when it's all over, brush them back and no one would ever notice. Poor fella so close all these years. Not two miles away from his parents, and they never knew. What's the world coming to?"

"History is rife with accounts of how badly people treat each other. Every generation thinks theirs is the worst. They're almost never right." Adriel knew this for a fact. "Ed, forgive me for asking such a personal question, but how is it that everyone thinks you're bedridden and here you are, clearly," Adriel waved a hand at him, "not."

"Can you keep a secret?"

"I don't lie." Can't would have been the more correct term.

"Fair enough. Everyone will find out soon enough, anyway. I wanted a vacation. Town politics can be so draining. After my heart attack, I thought I could do with a little less stress."

"How's that working out for you?" Adriel couldn't resist needling him a little. Ed's expression darkened.

"I'll just be on my way. Once again, I'd like to thank you for everything you did for Lydia. And for the lemonade." Cane thumping across the porch, Ed took his leave. Adriel watched the pinpoint of light until it was no longer visible before going back inside.

Chapter Eleven

"One of those strawberry cream-filled donuts and a cup of decaf." Adriel looked up to see a vision in white. Colonel Sanders style—complete with mustache, Panama hat, cane, and neck scarf. Kind eyes twinkled under bushy brows over a disarming smile. "You're new. I've never seen you here before." Adriel judged it would take at least fifteen years before he aged into being a dead ringer for the chicken guru. This man was still in the early salt and pepper stage.

"I'm Adriel."

"And you can forget hitting on her, you old rogue," Pam swung in from the back to tease her long-time customer. "She's got better sense than to be taken in by the likes of you." To Adriel, she said, "This is William Dooley. He's not half as charming as he likes to think."

"Nice to meet you." Adriel offered her hand in the traditional greeting, only to have him turn it over gently and kiss the back of it—the mustache bristled across her skin. *Not as soft as it looks*, she thought.

"Call me Bill."

Mr. Dooley carried his donut and coffee to the table by the window. Adriel felt his eyes resting on her from time to time while he ate slowly and with great relish. She didn't blame him; Wiletta made the strawberry cream from scratch. Eating one of those donuts was an extremely pleasurable experience.

Questions trembled on his tongue. The only one that made it to the surface was, "How do you find our little town, Adriel." He softened the A to an ah sound and rolled the R to make her name sound more exotic than it already was. "Quieter than where you're from?"

"Longbrook is a lovely place. I've grown quite fond of it over the past few weeks." Adriel deflected his attempt to pry information from her with a smile. "Did you grow up here?"

A shadow of strong emotion flitted over his features. If she hadn't been watching closely, she probably would have missed it. "Until I ran away to join the circus."

"The circus?" she repeated.

"Well, not exactly, but close. The rodeo came to town when I was but a callow youth with a few indiscretions in my past. I talked my way onto a bronc and found I had a knack for floating." A quirk of regret twisted his lips. "Sometimes running away is the same as running toward—if you get what I mean. My short career ended when I got freight-trained by a bull. Busted a hip that never healed right."

"Sounds like quite a story. Maybe you'll tell me about it in more detail sometime." She could relate to his logic when it came to running in any direction.

Pam called through from the kitchen. "Pry the top off that can of worms, and you'll be up to your ears in slimy wigglers before you can say 'rodeo clown'."

"Pipe down back there. It's not every day I get a set of new ears to bend with stories from my illustrious past." Bill softened the words with a smile.

"Tall tales, every one of them." Pam's voice held a hint of fondness. She stepped out of the kitchen to round the counter with a new pot of decaf. Bill's shoulders raised under the padded white of his suit jacket. Pam lifted the pot in an offer to top off his mug, but Bill laid a hand over it with a small shake of his head.

"Places to be." He turned to Adriel, "Miss Adriel, it was truly a pleasure to meet you. I'll be seeing you around." He

126

gulped the last of the coffee before making his way out the door.

She watched him pass by the window, leaning heavily on a polished black cane to help correct his uneven gait. Pam stepped up beside her to speak out of the corner of her mouth, "It's his story to tell—not that he's apt to trot the sordid parts of it out for you—but the way I heard it, it was more than a love for horses that dragged him out of town." Her cryptic comment piqued Adriel's interest, even though she preferred not to indulge in idle gossip. A short war between doing the right thing and prying information from Pam raged through her. Now she understood how easy it was to give in to temptation. The desire to hear everything Pam had to say was almost as strong as her distaste for talking about someone behind their back.

Pam's next words clinched Adriel's descent into sin.

"He left right after my brother went missing." A prickle of awareness raised gooseflesh on Adriel's arms. This was information she needed to hear. Pam had touched on the tragedy before. Now, Adriel hoped for more detail.

"Biggest mystery in Longbrook. My little brother went out for a ride on his bike and never returned. He was eight years old. Cute as a button and so sweet." Sorrow picked out the lines in Pam's face as she talked. "You hear about sibling rivalry, but for Ben and me it was never like that. The whole town searched for him for days. Weeks, really. No trace was ever found. After a while, the rumors started flying. He'd run away because my parents were abusing him; my mother killed him with a rolling pin and buried him in her tulip bed; and my personal favorite—I dared him to spend a night in the caves and he got lost." Adriel's intake of breath over this bit of cruelty was audible. Sneering scorn colored Pam's next words. "My father wanted to move away, but my mother and I were adamant we had to stay in case Bennie Boy ever came back. The stress took a toll on them both. I don't remember either of them ever smiling much after we lost him. It feels surreal to me knowing I don't have to wait anymore."

"What do you remember about that day?"

"I was grounded for fighting with my mother."

Adriel led Pam to a table. "Tell me everything. You'll feel better."

"It's funny. I'd forgotten until just now, but Bill was partly responsible for me getting into trouble. My best friend had this huge crush on him, and found out he and three of his buddies were planning a fishing trip up at the lake. Not that they'd have been doing any fishing. Everyone knew the only thing they ever pulled out of the water on those trips was another beer."

Confusion beetled Adriel's brows.

"Put the bottles in an old fishing trap and submerge it in the water. Keeps the beer cold." Pam explained, "Anyway, Sylvia talked me into playing the sleepover game with our folks. I'd say I was staying at her house; she'd say she was staying at mine; and we'd hitch a ride up to the lake to crash the fishing trip."

"I take it the ruse was ineffective."

"My mother called Sylvia's mother and we both got busted. Probably for the best anyway. Bill had a girlfriend, and, from what I heard, she was in trouble when he suddenly felt the lure of the rodeo. Might not have been true, though, since nine months came and went and there was no baby. Around this town, you can only believe half of what you hear and then you need to take that with a grain of salt."

"How far away is the lake?"

"Ten minute drive over a dirt road, if the weather's been dry. A little longer during rainy weather, or in spring when there are a lot of potholes. Why?"

"Just curious. Which direction is the lake? "

Pam's eyes widened. "It's up past the cabin. You really did land here right out of the blue, didn't you?"

"Something like that. Are all four of these men still living in the area?"

"Bill's still here; Graham Brier went off to college and got a job at an Internet startup right before it went big. I think he lives in Seattle now. Levi Hartman went into the Army and got himself killed in Afghanistan, which leaves Damien Oliver, who moved back to town last fall. You've met him, he runs the garage at the end of the street—eats lunch here every day."

Adriel filed the information away for future reference. She'd already spoken to Bill, and would make it a point to have a longer conversation with Damien. "I really am sorry for your loss." Adriel knew how lame the words sounded.

Pam's breath hitched, "Thirty years of not knowing he was right there the whole time. Two miles away from home. I thought it would feel different, you know? I thought finally learning what happened to him would be enough. I never expected to have to look at everyone I've known my whole life and wonder which one of them was the scumbag who killed my brother and didn't have the guts to come forward."

"Zack's a good cop. He'll get justice for Ben."

"He'll try, but he doesn't have a history here. I'm going to figure it out on my own." No one could be more devoted to solving the mystery than she would. Pam had no idea how invested Adriel was in securing Ben's future.

"I'll help."

"What?" Pam seemed skeptical.

"People talk to me. Since I'm new here, they all want to tell me their version of what happened back then. Maybe if we compare everyone's stories, we'll learn something new. For instance, he asked me not to say anything, but Edward showed up at my place last night."

"No." Pam pulled out a rag to wipe down the table. "Wait, isn't he bedridden?"

"Apparently not." Adriel recounted the conversation, complete with her impression that Ed hadn't been entirely truthful with her.

"If I'm right, the person who buried your brother has already killed again to keep his or her secret. Do you think it's safe for you to pry into the past like that?"

From the look on Pam's face, she hadn't put it together.

129

"Ooh, you mean Lydia. I thought you had a theory about her being killed to stop the ditch." Then it hit her, "Oh, you think whoever bashed her wanted to stop the ditch from going any further in order to keep Ben's bones from coming to light."

"The thought had occurred to me." Adriel's deadpan delivery made Pam lean back in her chair. She ran a hand through her disordered hair while it all fell into place. After a few moments of silence, she cast an enigmatic look at Adriel.

"You're hiding something from me. If you knew this was a possibility two weeks ago, then you had to have inside information." Watching Pam's attitude go from friendly to distrustful caused Adriel's stomach to drop into her shoes.

"There's…it's complicated."

Saved by the tinkling bell, Adriel hurried to wait on Mrs. Donato, who managed to collar Pam and cluck over the gruesome discovery. Finally escaping to the kitchen, Pam gave Adriel a pointed look that clearly said this talk wasn't over.

***

It came as no shock to Adriel when Pam burst through the cabin door ten minutes after Just Desserts closed for the day. She already had tea brewing—the loose type this time, not the kind in bags—and a pot of something called corn chowder on the stove. Having perused the many cookbooks left by Craig, it seemed the one recipe too easy for her to screw up.

With Estelle's agreement, she decided it was time to tell Pam the truth. So, when the woman in question stalked into the middle of the room and said, "You're going to tell me everything," Adriel held nothing back.

"Fine," she snapped, "I used to be a guardian angel. I tried to save one of my charges from crossing over before her time, and fell from heaven. Now I'm stuck in this…this human body, and I think I'm here to help your brother's spirit move on."

Pam's mouth dropped open, then snapped shut; her eyes narrowed, searched Adriel's for signs of mental instability. Adriel crossed her arms and stood staunchly defiant under Pam's piercing gaze.

"Why don't you join me for dinner, and I'll tell you about it," Adriel spoke softly, calmly.

Even if Pam thought her story was a load of something frequently found in a pasture, Adriel could tell she was willing to listen.

"But that's…" she began to protest.

"Crazy? Impossible?" Adriel filled in the sentence for her. "You think I don't know how it sounds?" The need for proof wrote itself all over Pam's face. "Remember the moment you first saw me."

Refusing to sit in the chair Adriel gestured toward, Pam paced as she replayed the entire scene in her mind. She saw the flash of angel wings, the outstretched hand; felt the truck stop when it should have continued forward. Brown eyes widened and glittered in her now-pale face.

"You," she pointed with a shaking hand but could not say more.

"Yes." For the first time all day, Adriel smiled. Secrets became a burden when not shared. "I am the angel Galmadriel." Her smile gave way to a frown, "Former angel. Or half angel, or something like it. That is the subject of much debate among my former brethren."

"I think I need to sit down for a minute. This is a lot to process." Pam's knees wobbled, but carried her the few steps to the table where she sat heavily. Adriel set a cup of tea in front of Pam and took the seat across the table. After a moment—and a sip of tea—Pam seemed to have regained some of her equilibrium.

Until she glanced around the room and her already pale face turned a sickly shade of gray.

"You're an angel, and I acted like I was doing you a favor to let you stay in this dump? I'm sorry. I had no idea. Well, you can't stay here."

The last thing Adriel expected was to be ousted and homeless again. Was this some kind of discrimination?

"My place isn't heaven, but it's better than this. We'll trade."

Oh.

"No, thank you, Pam. I'm fine here with the cat."

"Winston?"

"Yes, Winston. He's not especially talkative, though"

"You can talk to animals? That's a skill I'd love to have. Unless they talk all the time, and then it would probably get old really quickly." *Not as quickly as you will if you keep babbling like this*, the thought ran through Pam's head, *this is an angel you're boring to tears. Just shut up.*

Pam had no idea she'd spoken aloud, and Adriel bit her lip to keep from giving anything away.

Adriel couldn't help but smile when instead of shutting up, Pam's nerves took over and pushed her mouth into overdrive. For the next few minutes, she described her favorite childhood pet—a white cat with a black tail and two black spots on his head named Buttermilk, who had been both a confidant and boon companion. She avoided any mention of Ben.

Sensing the nervous energy behind Pam's spate of words, Adriel sipped her tea and patiently waited for her to push through the internal struggle to see the simple truth. Minute after minute filled with idle chatter, masking any notice of the elephant in the room

Finally, Pam managed to put a clamp on her case of verbal incontinence, and just stared at Adriel with questions in her eyes about what to do next.

"Let me get this straight. You're an angel in a human body, and no one up there can find anything better to have you do than live in this..." words failed her, so she just waved a hand to indicate the small space, "and sling pastries for barely more than tip money while you clear up a thirty-year-old mystery?"

132

Not auspicious, but that about sums it up. Adriel answered. "Yes."

"Can you..." Pam looked left then right and whispered, "Do stuff?"

"Stuff?"

"You know, like smite people?"

Adriel sighed. "No, and I don't play a harp, or wear a golden halo, either."

"Well, what can you do?"

"That is another topic of some debate. Angels can take on human form, but they remain beings of light—of energy—not of physicality. I'm the first one to ever be earthbound. I can tell you more things I can no longer do than things I can. That list is long and lamented. Oh, and my super power is killing electronics with nothing more than a glance."

"My GPS. Okay, I get why you don't drive. Or why you never answer your mobile." Adriel flashed Pam a grin.

"I've tried, but the minute I touch it, the batteries drain to nothing." A hint of bitterness crept in, "I'm useless."

"But you've talked to my brother, right? So you can see ghosts." It was a good point.

"Yes, I suppose I can. He's been with you all these years, if that helps."

"A little. I'm ashamed to say this, but I've had years to grieve, and as much as I miss him, knowing what happened has lifted a burden from me. I'd give anything to be able to see him one more time, so I envy you the ability; but there's also a sense of relief I'm unable to describe."

Leaving that line of conversation for another time and place, Adriel offered Pam a bowl of chowder while she questioned her more thoroughly about events on the day of Ben's accident.

Getting her secret out into the open eased something in Adriel. By the time their bowls were empty, they had the start of a timeline with as much detail as Pam could remember, and a plan to add to it.

On her way out the door, Adriel heard Pam mutter, "Oh, good Lord, I took an angel to a bra fitting."

"Good thing I can't smite people, isn't it?" Adriel called after her.

***

Over the next few days, Pam and Adriel fell into what was becoming their new routine of eating breakfast together and trading information. Pam placed a plate of something that looked like a slice bread cooked in some kind of coating in front of Adriel, and drizzled it with deeply amber maple syrup. The dish smelled intoxicating.

"What's this called?"

"French toast." Pam's face tried to frown and smile at the same time. Even though Adriel thought Pam had believed her story, the occasional doubt surfaced. Moments like these put those doubts to rest. She whispered to Adriel, "Don't they have food in heaven? I'm rethinking whether I want to go there if I can't eat all the chocolate and pastries I want and not gain weight."

"Not every angel has taken on a human lifetime. I had no idea how satisfying food could be until now." The answer to her question was quite a lot more complex than that, but there was a code to follow. Humans should not have too much information about their final destination.

With the finding of Ben's remains being the talk of the town, it was easy enough for Adriel to mine customers for information, and for Pam to do the same. When Callum walked into Just Desserts, Pam sidled up to Adriel, waggled her eyebrows and added a hint of suggestiveness, "Maybe you could interrogate him." A stricken look crossed her face. "Oh, no. That was inappropriate, wasn't it? Do angels, you know…"

Adriel wasn't sure she did know, so she twirled a hand to indicate Pam should explain.

Pam's voice dropped to a whisper, "Sex." Adriel's face went red and hot.

"I'm familiar with the concept." The absolute dryness in her tone shut the conversation down—partly to keep from having to examine the purely physical impulses Callum had raised in her, and partly to keep from giving away information Pam should not be privy to in the first place.

***

Everything Adriel had experienced over the past few weeks made her rethink her attitude toward humans. In a case of outright snobbery, she had neglected to consider how many factors played on the emotions. Some physical; some mental. When she began experiencing an overwhelming desire to return to Oakville, at first she chalked it up to some kind of hormonal influence, and did her best to ignore the mounting pressure.

Although Estelle was sure he was fine, Julius had not returned since the day the dark entity sent him away. Neither of her erstwhile guardians responded to her calls, which was highly frustrating. Their prolonged absence planted seeds of suspicion that one of both of them might be behind the compulsion. In the end, Adriel gave in and started looking for a means of transportation. Driving a car was out since Pam knew better than to loan hers, and Adriel had no one else to ask.

One of Craig's boxes contained a map of the state that showed Adriel just how disconcertingly close Oakville was to her present location. A mere twelve miles. Even if she could convince one of her friends to give her a ride back, that was a long walk.

Remembering Pam's advice to stick to riding a bike, and Craig's affinity for keeping everything he ever owned, checking the as-yet unexplored shed in the corner of the property was probably going to be her best bet. The idea of going in there, though, gave her pause. Adriel had nothing against spiders. It was their homes she could do without—particularly when it came to wearing bits of said homes, along with their inevitable cargo of dead bug parts, anywhere on her person.

Her expectations were met when she yanked the door open to see an absolute wall of yuck. This was worse than the lean-to shed where she'd found the yard implements. So, saying an apology to all eight-legged beasties within hearing distance, she taped a flashlight to the handle of an old broom—light pointing bristle-ward—and swept down every sticky, dusty web barring her way.

There was a moment of regret for opportunities lost as she stumbled over a gas-powered lawn mower that would have made her life a lot easier these past few weeks. Surprisingly, the area contained less clutter than the cabin. And an old car.

Adriel's unwillingness to drive didn't mean she knew nothing about cars. This thing, however, barely qualified. Only when she squinted could she pick out the make and model. As best as she could tell, it was a 1970's era Frankenmobile. The main body was a Buick Skylark. Adriel could tell because it was the 1972 Suncoupe model that featured a retractable canvas sunroof. The rest of it, though, was a mix and match of parts. Pontiac LeMans fenders, doors from a Chevelle, and the rear clip had come from an Olds Grand Prix. None of the trim matched up anywhere, and every part of the car was a different color. As a finishing touch, the previous owner had bolted on a hood ornament off a '56 Chevy. A heavy layer of dust coated the chrome, and it was pitted in a few spots, but she admired the sleek lines of the aircraft in flight. Even in its current state, the car had nice lines.

But she wasn't here to look at a car, she was here to find a bicycle.

Just when it seemed her efforts had been fruitless, the beam of light picked out a flash of red from a reflector affixed to the bumper of a vintage Schwinn. From the teasing glimpse

Adriel managed at this distance, the bike appeared to be blue, with a two-tone saddle seat, and white sidewall tires. Some rusty old farm implements blocked the Schwinn from an easy trip back to daylight, but Adriel was determined to release it from its cage of darkness.

As she reached for the first obstacle—something with pointy tines curved into large C shapes—she heard a voice behind her drawl, "I hope your Tetanus shot is up to date."

Whirling, she glared at Callum. "Sneaking up on me like that when I have a weapon in my hand is not a good idea."

"What were you going to do? Sweep me to death? Blind me with the flashlight?"

Despite her annoyance, his question drew a wry smile.

"Maybe," she brandished the broom, "I should warn you, this thing's loaded."

"With cobwebs. I think I'll take my chances," he scoffed.

"Did you come in here to help, or just to state the obvious? It seems to be your biggest talent." She really wanted to get that bike out of its cocoon and see what shape it was in.

Callum refrained from answering and, with a ripple of muscle that drew a sigh from Adriel's lips for some reason she wasn't quite sure she understood, lifted the many-tined whatsit out of the way as though it weighed no more than a feather. Just as quickly, he dispatched each remaining obstacle before flexing again to lift the dusty blue bike and carry it outside.

"Nice shape for its age."

"It seems sturdy enough."

"Tires have a little dry rot, but I think there's another set hanging on a nail back there. Might be newer." Adriel watched him disappear back into the shed, her eyes lingering on the planes of his broad shoulders. The sound of something falling followed by a couple of nasty words prompted her to call out to see if he had been hurt.

"I'm fine. One sec." He emerged from the shed holding a pair of tires in one hand and an extra set of tubes in the other. "Got them. Let's have a look." Callum laid one tire up against the bike and passed the other through his hand to check for cracks.

"Well?" Adriel said when he was through.

"They'll do. I saw a pump hanging on the wall by the workbench." He pulled out a multi-use pocket knife and used one of the implements to let the remaining air out of the inner tube. "Go get it, would you?" The order was tossed carelessly over his shoulder.

Adriel watched with fascinated interest as Callum set to work wrestling the old tires from the rims. He used a pair of screwdrivers to pry the rubber away from the spoked metal, then reversed the process after tucking a new inner tube into place.

About ten minutes into the job, he muttered, "Be nice if someone offered me a cold drink." Chagrined, Adriel realized she had forgotten her manners. There was a pitcher of sun tea brewing on the porch; by the color she judged it strong enough, and quickly dosed it with ice, a little lemon, and just enough sugar to take the bitterness away. She poured two glasses and returned to where Callum was just beginning to pry the second tire from the rim.

"Would you like a cold drink?" Her tone was sweeter than the tea, but with an edge of sarcasm.

"Yes, thanks." Callum stood, stripped off his shirt, then rubbed the cool glass across his forehead. Adriel's mouth went dry at the sight, and to make matters worse, she gulped down too much iced tea and nearly choked. Luckily, Callum had already turned back to his task and didn't notice.

"There, I think the old girl still has some life in her."

"Thank you for all your hard work."

"She's almost ready to go. One more thing and you'll be able to test her out."

"Maybe later," Adriel reached for the bike, "It needs a good cleaning first."

"*She*," he emphasized, "is just a little dusty." For lack of anything else handy, he swiped his own tee shirt over the bike.

"She? How does an inanimate object develop a gender?"

"No idea. Just the way it is." Callum called back over his shoulder as he disappeared into the shed again to return seconds later with a small oil can. The chain and sprockets received a liberal anointing with the smelly contents while he lifted the rear tire off the ground and had Adriel spin the pedal. "Take her for a spin." After a few revolutions, the wheel spun free and easy. Callum had her test the brakes by reversing the pedal. They worked like a charm.

"Maybe later." *After you've gone.*

"You do know how to ride a bike don't you?"

The lie trembled on her lips but would not pass them. "No. But I'm sure I can figure it out all on my own. Surely it can't be that difficult a thing to learn. Children do it every day."

The way his eyes lit up, Adriel knew she was in trouble. Flipping up the kickstand, he gestured for her to take her place on the seat. Half a zillion thoughts chased through Adriel's head, and not a single valid excuse among them.

"It's all about balance and momentum. Put your feet on the pedals and I'll give you a push to get started."

"There's no need..."

"Hold onto the handlebars and if you want to stop, just turn the pedals backwards. This model isn't equipped with hand brakes." Every attempt to deflect his help went ignored.

She sent up a prayer that she wouldn't tip over in front of him, and felt his hand brush her backside as he grasped the seat to help guide her forward. Distracted by the tingling from the point of contact, she wobbled the handlebars when the bike started to move.

"Pedal."

Callum's shouted command startled Adriel's feet into motion. With a mighty shove, he propelled her down the drive while she pedaled madly until she felt the rhythm click into place and everything smoothed out. Leaning into the motion, she felt the wind rush past cheeks sore from smiling. This was more fun than she ever expected. Sometimes being human wasn't half bad.

At the end of the drive, Adriel completed a turn that was only a little shaky, and pedaled back toward the man who grinned back at her.

"Not bad for your first time."

"Faint praise, but I'll take it. Thank you for…well, everything."

"Pay me back by letting me take you to dinner."

"How would that be paying you back? I don't follow your logic." And she suspected there were undercurrents of human interaction here that she wasn't able to understand. Oddly, a memory from a recent movie marathon with Pam provided the answer as Adriel searched her mind for context. "A date?" Her shocked tone turned the half-grin on his face into a toothy smile.

"Now you're catching on. I just want to get to know you better. Over dinner."

Her angel past and her human present started a full-on battle over whether dating was something either of them should be doing, while Callum waited with an amused expression on his face as though he could see her internal struggle.

Human beat angel, which, she supposed, spoke volumes about how free will actually works. It was a bad idea, and she didn't care, because she felt drawn to him in ways that had everything to do with hormones.

"Okay, but I get to choose the venue."

"Pick you up at seven?"

"Tomorrow night. I've got something I need to do today."

"Pick someplace nice, okay?"

"I've already decided. Athena's."

"You're killing me, Angel."

A shiver ran through her.

***

The sharp smell of grease assaulted Adriel's nose through the open garage bay door as she wheeled the bike toward Damien Oliver.

"I was hoping you might have a minute to check my bike over before I take it out for a spin."

"Sure. Just give me a second." An air wrench bucked to life with a high-pitched whirring sound when he applied it to the last two lug nuts on a rusty pickup truck. While she waited, Adriel glanced with interest at the organized chaos around her. Tools spilled out of wheeled metal boxes and across his workbench.

"Okay, let's have a look. Is this Craig's old Schwinn?"

"It is. Pam suggested I pull it out of storage and give it some use. If you think it's road worthy, that is. I could use a long ride after all the commotion out at my place lately." For a split second, Damien froze. Adriel only caught the slight pause because she was watching his reaction closely.

"Shame about what happened," he changed the subject. "You don't have to worry about anything, bike's safe as houses."

"You must have been around when Ben went missing, what's your theory?"

"It was an accident. Had to be. No one in this town would deliberately kill a kid. You're all set now, is there anything else I can do for you?"

"How much do I owe you?" Adriel couldn't tell if he was rushing her out because he had too much work, or if he didn't want to talk about Ben anymore.

"No charge." He gave her a wide smile, then flipped the handle on the lift to lower the pickup while Adriel rode away, unsure whether she had learned anything or not.

Chapter Twelve

Rough-textured floorboards chafed at her bare feet when Adriel stepped onto the porch, a steaming cup of mediocre coffee in her hand. Early morning sun teased a pleasant heat from the boards that would later in the day turn too warm to navigate without shoes. When her foot unexpectedly came down on something alive and moving, Adriel jumped halfway out of her skin, but managed to keep the shriek from escaping her lips. A mouse no bigger than a walnut scurried under the chair to peer back at her with accusing eyes.

"Sorry, didn't see you."

The tiny creature limped out from the shadows, his left hind foot cocked at an odd angle.

"Did I do that to you?" Poor thing. Did he just shake his head? It must have been her imagination. "Well, come on, then. Let's have a look." The mouse willingly scampered onto Adriel's outstretched hand, where he sat impassively while she poked and prodded. At her gentle touch on his injured foot, a tingle passed from her to him. The foot straightened and healed. If only she had more control of the power Estelle assured her she still retained. Maybe someday.

"I'm going to put you back in the field and you're going to stay outside." A wagging finger emphasized her point. "Your bathroom habits aren't fit for indoor living."

Sharing a home with Winston, even if he refused to talk to her, was one thing—and while she loved the little creatures of the world, she preferred not to live with all of them. Anything that poops while it eats was not on her list of potential housemates.

While she talked to him, the bright little mouse sat on her hand, his beady eyes brimming with humor—okay, you have to look for it in animals, but it's there—and with her attention focused on him, Adriel totally missed seeing or hearing Callum until he spoke.

"Good morning, Snow White. Or, would that be Adriel Doolittle?"

It took a second to leaf through her mental catalog for the reference. Snow White. Disney movie adapted from a fairy tale. The main character talked to animals. Dr. Doolittle, also made into a movie and he also talked to animals. Got it.

"Most creatures are friendly if you approach them gently." Sweeping past him and down the steps, Adriel relished the sensation on her bare feet as she crossed the cooler, slightly damp grass to let the mouse go at the edge of the field. Callum caught the double meaning easily enough, and she felt his amused gaze on her.

"Oh, I can be plenty gentle if you've a mind to get friendly." His voice, low and smooth, cruised over her nerves to send them jangling into alarm mode. Her response to him had to be a sign that he was dangerous in some capacity she didn't quite understand.

"Yes, well." Adriel's noncommittal reply, meant to dissuade him from pursuing the conversation, failed utterly, and when she turned back, his body blocked the steps. To go back inside meant brushing past him—maybe even touching him. She shivered at the thought. "I'm partial to furry companions. Thanks anyway."

Callum's knowing grin told her she'd made another conversational gaffe. Talking to him was like walking through a minefield of potential double entendres. For once, he decided to let it go and changed the subject. He wandered over toward the trench with yellow and black tape still fluttering around it.

144

"Shame about Ben. Dying all alone like that." He sounded genuinely concerned, which surprised Adriel into doing the math. Callum and Ben would have been of a similar age. If Callum grew up here, they probably had been friends.

"Did you know him?"

"It's a small town. Everyone knows everyone. He was a couple years behind me in school, but we were friends." she heard the pain behind the simple statement.

"Were you surprised to think he might have run away from home?"

"I never bought that story for a minute. No one with half a brain and eyes in their head would have. Ben and his family were tight, and he wasn't the kind of kid to get into trouble. Rodeo Bill started those rumors back in the day." Callum spit the words out like a condemnation—and like there was more he could say, but chose not to.

"Rodeo Bill? I've met him. He seems like quite a character." Wanting to hear more, Adriel gestured for Callum to take a seat in one of the chairs on the porch, then lowered herself into the other.

"That's one word for it. The Allens got a raw deal. Some folks turned on them, and others turned their backs in case the stigma of losing a kid was somehow catching. I know my mother was paranoid for months. No one asked us kids what we thought happened."

"Children often see more than adults credit them for. I'd be interested to hear your thoughts on the subject."

"We figured he'd gone exploring and gotten lost. There's a set of caves up on the hill that were off-limits, but we used to sneak up there anyway. A kid could get stuck in the smaller tunnels where an adult would never fit. Bunch of us kept searching long after there was any chance he could have survived. I guess we figured if we found a body, at least we could bring him home." It haunted Callum—the lack of closure and the thought of Ben trapped under the ground alone. Learning Ben's whereabouts after all this time raised a lot of questions.

As though talking about him had called Ben to them, Adriel heard the card on bicycle spokes rising above the sounds of singing birds and buzzing insects. Her eyes flicked past Callum to note the small figure pedaling furiously toward the cabin.

Ben fishtailed into the yard and jumped off the seat with excited energy. "I remembered something," he shouted. "Right before I...before it happened, I looked over my shoulder and saw a plane. Who's that?" Ben didn't recognize Callum.

Thinking fast, Adriel figured out a way to answer the question without speaking out of turn, "I'm sure Ben would appreciate how hard you and your friends worked at trying to find him, Callum."

Registering surprise, Ben said, "Callum? He's Callum McCord? He's old."

"It's his sister I feel sorry for the most. For thirty years she's lived with innuendo and suspicion. Woman's got guts to stay here and face that kind speculation. Anyone with a lick of common sense knew his family never hurt that boy, but that didn't stop the talk."

"People can be cruel." No one knew that better than Adriel. An eternity of watching some of the things humans chose to do to each other might have left her thinking the species was beyond redemption—if not for the numerous acts of shining kindness they were prone to as well. "Most of the time, cruelty is born of fear."

"Maybe so."

The moment spun out. Ben standing at the edge of the porch, face sober as he processed the information Callum had inadvertently provided—Callum falling silent while he remembered a boy gone far too soon. Words failed Adriel. Nothing she could say to either of them would make this easier. Only time had the power to heal all wounds.

***

The sound of raised, angry voices once again penetrated Adriel's sleep. What was it with this place? Wearily, she sat up in bed and twitched the curtain aside to see what was going on now.

Half a dozen citizens carrying signs blocked Gideon and his crew from gaining access to their equipment. Too tired to care whether or not her clothes matched, Adriel threw on the first items that came to hand—a floral top over a striped skirt in clashing colors, and jammed her feet into two different styles of flip flops. Gustavia would have been so proud.

Behind her, the screen door creaked and slammed as footsteps heavy with frustration fell across the porch. Enough. She had had enough. Righteous indignation carried her right into the middle of the two groups.

"Give it a rest. For the love of all that's holy. All I want to do is wake up to the sound of rain on the roof or birds singing. Do you people really think this is the way to handle things?" She rounded on the sign carriers led by Rodeo Bill. "It's been three weeks of constant racket disturbing my sleep and look," dramatic arm wave, "they're almost done. You're too late to stop this, and really, what is the point? All you are doing is delaying the work and costing more time and money. Go home. Or maybe you'd prefer if Zack Roman came out to take all your fingerprints? Someone should be held accountable for the damage they're trying to fix. Go home and let these men do their jobs." A hint of angel slid through her voice, making the command more powerful. After a short burst of protest and a few sidelong glances at the irate redhead, the picketers looked toward Rodeo Bill to signal their next move. He rounded on Adriel, and what she saw was unexpected.

Bill was scared. The signs were subtle, but they were there: slightly elevated breathing; eyes blinking rapidly; white knuckles clutching his sign; and tight shoulders. He opened his mouth to say something, thought better of it, then turned and walked away. Subtle changes in his posture suggested defeat. The others followed while Adriel looked after Bill thoughtfully. Something was going on with him, and she meant to find out what.

Chapter Thirteen

The last two-mile stretch into Oakville marked the beginning of a gradual uphill climb that turned Adriel's legs to noodles and dried her mouth. Why hadn't she had the foresight to bring along some bottled water? Some mean trick of the light made the crest of the hill seem closer than it was. Eventually, out of necessity, she stood to put more pressure on the pedals until even with the extra force, she had to get off the bike and push it the last few hundred feet. Parts of her lower anatomy felt rubbed raw from the edges of the seat, her hands stung where they grasped the rubber grips, and she wished she could heal herself so she didn't have to spend the next few days sitting on a cushion.

Nestled against the lower edge of a lake big enough to provide plenty of boating and fishing, the town of Oakville bustled during the tourist months. Striped awnings shaded shop windows from the glare of sun off the water, and brightly colored umbrellas covered picnic table seating along a series of sun-whitened piers.

Wind roughened cedar siding festooned with fishing nets and floats contrasted with lighter, more colorful trim to continue the seaside theme. Out on the lake, triangle sails caught subtle air currents to pull their cargo through the rippling blue. The temptation to whiz down the hill and right into that cool, clear moisture was hard to resist. Instead, Adriel set her sights on the tiny yellow building with the big plastic ice cream cone attached to the roof. A scoop of double chocolate chip would go down good right about now.

The damp breeze off the water smelled like fresh rain and sunshine with the faintest hint of fish. Had there been any skin left on her abraded behind, Adriel would have wanted to sit and bask there for hours. As it was, she needed to put the last leg of the trip behind her to get to Hayward House. If Julie wasn't home, she was sunk. Adriel jammed all thought of the trip back home into the farthest, darkest corner of her mind where she hoped it would die of neglect. Lifting her leg over the saddle proved impossible so she pushed the bike past a knot of tourists chattering loudly about who was at fault for making them late to meet their boat charter.

Too busy listening to the lively discussion, Adriel nearly plowed into the peacock-bright figure that appeared in front of her.

"Adriel? Is that you?" Gustavia reached out to steady the bike when it bobbled in Adriel's startled grip. "Did you ride all the way here?"

Adriel winced before she could stop herself. "Yes, I did." One hand dropped to absently rub her sore backside, causing a shiver of pain.

"That's it. You're coming with me." Gustavia commandeered the bike to wheel it around the ice cream place toward the dead-end block where Kat lived. Long legs flashing, she took off like a rocket while Adriel, feeling as if she had aged fifty years in the last five minutes, limped along behind. The longer she stayed off the bike, the more stiff her legs became.

"You couldn't have come at a better time," Gustavia called back over her shoulder, "We're having a sample party over at Kat's this afternoon."

"Oh, I don't want to intrude." Ignoring the shriek of protest from her calf muscles, Adriel dashed forward to wrest the Schwinn from Gustavia's hands. "I'll just ride back to…"

"Honey, not even Amethyst is foolish enough to take bets on whether or not you could ride that bike fifty feet, much less make it back to Longbrook. You'll come to Kat's with me, and we'll see what we can do to fix you up." Her gaze brushed over Adriel, taking in the stiffened gait, chafed hands, and expression that became more pained with every step. "Painkillers, liniment, and a dose of Amethyst will go a long way to putting you right. One of us will give you a ride home, too."

Too tired to argue, and thankful Kat lived nearby, Adriel followed Gustavia the scant distance to the small, but cheerful yellow and white house. The thought of asking what was a *sample party* never even crossed Adriel's mind as Gustavia leaned the bike up against the porch and hustled her inside.

"Hey, where is everyone?" She called out. "Guess who's here."

"Kitchen."

It turned out that a sample party involved a dozen or so cup-sized containers of wall paint and an equal number of disposable brushes. Several swatches of color already decorated each wall of the kitchen so Kat could choose between them. All but two selections had been x'ed out. There was so much color in the smallish room already that the samples were all but swallowed up in the visual frenzy. When Kat's grandmother, the original Madame Zephyr—medium and fortune teller—died, she passed down more than just her famed psychic gifts. Kat also inherited this house, complete with a kitchen full of china teapots. In every shade and pattern, they squatted on shelves, the tops of the cabinets, and filled a built in breakfront with enough bright color to assault the eye.

"Adriel. Welcome." Kat and Julie offered warm hugs while Amethyst scanned her aura.

"What have you done to yourself?" Eyes slightly unfocused, Amethyst ran gentle fingers over Adriel's auric energy field. Every now and then, she stopped to twitch at specific areas and flick her fingers as though throwing something away. With each tweak, the pain and stiffness lessened.

"She rode an old bike over here," Gustavia answered, since Adriel wasn't capable at that point of stringing two words together. The power rolling off the diminutive, purple-clad woman had soothed her into a trance-like state. Maybe all those worries over Amethyst had been for nothing. In the short time since events had caused her aura-reading ability to level up to the nth degree, Amethyst had taken command of her new strength without any help at all. Adriel wanted to be bitter about it, but with peace flooding over her, she couldn't muster up the angst.

When Amethyst drew back her energy, Adriel swayed on her feet.

"Wow." Not the most angelic of statements, but it was the only word that came to mind.

Julie pressed an over-sized mug of tea into Adriel's hand. "Ammie can really turn it on when she needs to. How do you feel?"

"Better. Much better." The spicy, slightly medicinal-tasting brew smoothed out the rest of the rough edges.

"Take these," Kat pressed two tablets into Adriel's hand. "You'll be right as rain in a few minutes." Eyes sparkling under a dark fringe of bangs, she waited until Adriel downed the pills, then gestured toward the walls. "It's a good thing you showed up; we need a tie-breaker. We can't decide between that sage green with yellow and gray accents, or the cream with russet and blue."

"That one." Adriel pointed to the more neutral selection. "It works with all the colors and patterns in the room."

"See, that's what I said." Julie pulled the brush from the pot of green and drew a circle around that combination. "Okay, that's one room down." She bobbed her head toward the newcomer, "With her here, we might actually get through this and be ready for the painters."

"When are they coming?" Adriel was curious.

"Tomorrow." It was a chorus of voices.

"Ah, I see. Nothing like leaving things until the last minute."

"Snarky," Amethyst's husky voice held a laugh. "I approve."

Now that she was here, where a sense of peace flowed over her, the compulsion Adriel had been feeling faded away. Spending time with these women—women who knew her deepest secret and spared her the searching looks because they accepted her—healed something Adriel hadn't known was broken. Their compassion for her came from the wisdom gained during their own struggles with self-acceptance. While Adriel, in her capacity as guardian angel, had been assigned to watch over Amethyst during the past year, she'd had a ringside seat when each woman had been put to the test.

Pulling her attention back to the present, Adriel chimed in on the raging debate over an appropriate color for Kat's reading room. Nestled into the sunny spot created by a set of bay windows, a polished table and two chairs took up the most of the room. Seven sample colors marched across the table's top. No wonder Kat couldn't choose.

"The deep blue simply screams psychic," Adriel's tongue might have been firmly planted in her cheek, but the thread of truth in the words sent Gustavia into a fit of giggles.

"Yellow it is, then." Kat decided firmly. "I prefer to avoid cliches when it comes to my line of work."

"There are two shades of yellow. Which one?"

"That one." Four voices chimed at once. Another tie.

"Then I get to decide, right?" Adriel established the parameters. Kat circled a hand to indicate she should get on with it. "Well, I choose this," she passed over both pots of yellow and held up a medium gray with just enough hints of warmth to contrast nicely with the white trim and still work well with the tones in the kitchen.

"I love it, and I'm putting you in charge. Here's the box, and here's your crown." Kat plopped a white paper painter's cap over Adriel's titian hair. Amethyst pulled a ten out of her pocket; handed it over to Kat with a sigh. "Might as well give this to you now. There's no way it's going past midnight with her in charge." She cocked a thumb at Adriel.

An hour and a half later, Kat was the owner of a box of marked samples, a second box of rejects, and a completed chart listing all the color combinations.

"This calls for a celebration. It's not even dark out yet ,and we're done. I was sure we were still going to be arguing when the painters showed up in the morning," Kat said.

"Then why did you bet me we'd be done before midnight?" Amethyst sent Kat a mock glare. No matter how many bets they made, Kat always won. They made so many that, paradoxically, Gustavia and Julie had bet on whether or not Kat and Ammie would bet.

"Red or white?" Amethyst's question sailed right over Adriel's head. She frowned her ignorance.

"What kind of wine do you like? Red or white?"

"Oh. I don't have a favorite." It wasn't exactly a lie, but it was close enough to trigger a second blurt, "I've never had wine before." The words hit Adriel's ears at the same time as the others heard them. It was becoming clear to her that lying, in any form, was not on her list of abilities.

"Give her the red," Julie said.

Nose wrinkling at what she perceived as a rotten fruit smell, Adriel took a cautious sip of the ruby liquid. It tasted better than it smelled. She drank a little more and felt the burn of alcohol in the back of her throat. With half a glass gone, she felt a case of the giggles coming on. How undignified. She bit down on the urge to laugh, and something between a snort and a twitter emerged—which might have been fine except the current topic of conversation didn't involve anything humorous.

All eyes turned toward her. "I think Adriel is drunk," Kat's glance took in the glass in her hand. "On half a glass of wine."

"Must be an angel thing," Adriel's own comment set her off on another round of giggling. "Or something to do with spirits." Her play on words missed the mark. "You know…alcohol is sometimes called spirits, and so are ghosts,

and I work with ghosts. Oh, come on. It's a pun. It's funny."
Apparently it wasn't. "Tough crowd."

No wonder people sometimes struggled with alcohol addiction—Adriel couldn't remember feeling this good since taking on flesh. Inhibitions siphoned away in a liquid rush that left her feeling oddly lighter than before.

Her eyes had dropped closed while she savored the sensation. When they popped open again she was looking at four astonished faces.

"Something wrong?" How could feeling this good be wrong?

"Look." Gustavia turned Adriel toward the mirror where a familiar face looked back at her.

"What?"

"What do you mean, what? Don't you see it?"

Leaning closer, Adriel peered at her reflection. Jet black hair in a pixie cut curled around heavily pierced ears. Blood red lipstick smeared over pouted lips below dark-rimmed eyes that stared back at her with just a hint of insolence from the palest of faces. "Do I have lipstick on my teeth?" She bared her teeth to make sure.

"Adriel! You didn't look like that when you came in here."

Her befuddled brain refused to process the concept. This was one of her many bodies—the one she used when relating to angst-ridden charges in the throes of their teen years. What was the big deal?

Gustavia did something completely unexpected; she reached out and pinched Adriel on the upper arm. Hard. Hard enough to leave a mark.

"Ow!" Adriel rubbed the spot and glared at her pincher. "What was that for?"

"Because you need to sober up and catch a clue. You totally changed bodies right in front of us."

"I did?" Well, duh, of course she had. "So what? Angels can appear in any form. That's nothing new."

155

And then it hit her. "Oh." She shook her finger at the image in the mirror. "Oh." Shock registered roundly in the eyes staring back from the silvered glass. "Oh." Clothing hung oddly on this much smaller frame. She looked like a child playing dress up. A fairly apt description of her life if she wanted to get philosophical about it. Sad, really.

This had disaster written all over it. In big, black, permanent marker.

All the giddy lightness drained out of her just as quickly as it had come.

"What am I going to do if I stay stuck in this body?"

"You won't." Amethyst's face appeared in the mirror. "The wine relaxed you, lowered your inhibitions and released you from limiting beliefs."

"So, I should drink more? That seems like a self-destructive course of action."

"Did I say that? No. You just need to let go of personal misconceptions. Before today—tell the truth—you thought you couldn't alter the face you present to the world."

Adriel's expression answered for her.

"Now you know you can. All you have to do is recreate whatever you were feeling when it happened. Close your eyes and think back to that moment."

Amethyst was right, in theory. Her plan, though, left a lot of room for doubt and fear. What if changing worked, but only for a different form? What if it didn't? Tension twanged Adriel's muscles into ropy tightness that refused to relax.

"It's not working." Five times of squeezing her eyes and wrinkling her nose in concentration proved fruitless. Every time she looked into the mirror, Miss teenage Goth stared back at her.

"You think we need to get her drunk again?" A tiny smile accompanied Julie's otherwise serious question.

"We'll save it as a last resort," Amethyst replied dryly.

"Probably wouldn't work anyway." Adriel's sullen tone matched her face, which seemed to be fixed in a permanent sneer.

"Give her a few minutes to get her thoughts settled." Gustavia slung an arm around Adriel, pulled her away from the mirror, and settled with her on the sofa. "There's no pressure right now. You're among friends who know you for what's beneath the skin." Her voice modulated into a soothing tone while she ran a hand gently back and forth over Adriel's forearm. "Let's not think about it for a little while; see what happens. Kat, why don't you put in a video? Something light and funny. We'll have popcorn and a few laughs. There's time enough to deal with this later. Our work is done; let's just have a girl's night. It's been awhile since we've had one of those."

Panic settled from world-shaking to a quivering tremor under Gustavia's calming touch. Amethyst and Kat went into the kitchen to prepare snacks and whisper where Adriel couldn't hear, while Julie pawed through Kat's movie collection looking for something suitably lighthearted.

Another cup of soothing tea accompanied the popcorn in an odd but surprisingly satisfying combination, but it wasn't the tea or even more alcohol that eventually did the trick. It was a bout of belly-shaking laughter over Gustavia and Kat acting out scenes from Notting Hill in fake British accents that finally relaxed Adriel.

In a rush, the tension washed away taking both inner and outer Goth along for the ride.

"And she's back." Amethyst, hyper-aware of the energy around her, saw it happen out of the corner of her eye. "Your aura is a lot lighter than it was before, too."

"Can you do it again? On purpose, I mean." Julie voiced the question uppermost in Adriel's mind.

"I can try." Closing her eyes, she concentrated on accessing the calm place from moments before. Nothing happened. It was as though a glass wall separated her from the seat of her power. She could see it pulsing like a live thing, but could not touch it while the barrier held. "No. The power is there, but I can't use it."

"Have you been in contact with other angels? What do they say about your situation?"

Julie's direct question posed a dilemma for Adriel. How should she answer? Since lying hadn't gone so well for her up until now, she decided to stick to the truth.

"I've been assigned a pair of guardians since my situation seemed to need more than just one. I think you might know them."

"Grams and Julius? Yes, we know."

"You know? How could that possibly be? I didn't find out until I'd been here a week."

Julie exchanged a sidelong glance with Kat. "They were with us when we found the last cache. We saw them become angels right before this booming voice told them you had fallen and it was up to them to look after you."

The explanation had a very different effect on Adriel than expected. She levered off the sofa to rant.

"Well isn't that just dandy. Humans knowing angel business…and I'm left in the dark. No one tells me anything anymore, and I'm sick of it. There are rules. I followed those rules. Okay, maybe not there at the end, but still…you can't tell me I was a bad angel. I took good care of my charges. Amethyst can tell you." While Adriel worked herself up, a familiar prickling sensation stole over the women who watched. "…tell me I'm an angel in a human body then treat me like an outcast. I've had just about enough of this."

Adriel paced like a caged animal. "Estelle, you show yourself right now! I know how this works, don't act like you can't hear me when I know you can."

The prickling increased. "See, I can feel you there. Show yourself!"

"That's enough!" Estelle's voice boomed, though she did not show herself as ordered.

"Oh, it's not even close to enough. I have questions and I want answers. Don't tell me I am still an angel and treat me like a mortal."

"Then stop acting like one. I don't have time to hold your hand right now. Julius is missing, and the council seems to think you're the only one who can help me find him. In order

158

for you to do that, you're going to have to get over this ridiculous identity crisis. So, from one angel to another, I'm telling you to suck it up and find a way to be helpful." Estelle withdrew her energy.

"Did she just tell me to suck it up?" Adriel slumped back into her spot next to Gustavia on the sofa. Amethyst read both astonishment and chagrin in the shifting colors of her aura.

"I believe she did." The part about Julius was concerning, but Kat couldn't help finding Estelle's choice of phrase amusing. "What are you going to do about it?"

To everyone's surprise, Adriel burst into tears. "It's my fault. I think I know what happened to Julius, and every one of you is in danger, too." Through her sobs, she told the others what had happened on the day she had last spoken with Julius. She sensed Estelle listening in, too.

"I thought we got rid of Billy when we sent him down to the dark. Was it all for nothing?"

"No. Don't say that." Kat admonished Julie for speaking out in such bitter tones. "We did what we had to do, and if we need to do it again, then sign me up."

"It wasn't Billy. You need to think this through carefully. I know your first instinct is to help, but whatever took Julius is so much more dangerous than Billy ever was. I hope Estelle is wrong. Not about there being a chance of getting him back, but about me being the one to make it happen."

"Pity party much?" Amethyst lost her patience. "If that's the way you want to play it, then fine, but before you do, there's something I want to show you." The fairy-like woman concentrated for a moment then held up both hands toward Adriel. The taller woman's eyes rolled back in her head when the force of the reader's vision hit her. Only for a second, and then she saw what Amethyst wanted to show her.

Wings.

A glorious set of wings unfurled behind her and looked so real Adriel could almost feel their weight against her shoulders. Her breath caught and held. Oh, but they were beautiful. Almost as beautiful as the light that formed a corona around her body. This was her truest self, or it had been before the fall. How cruel of Amethyst to show her what she'd lost.

"For someone who is supposed to be a higher being, you sure can be dumb at times. This is you. Now. Not before the fall. Now. Look more closely." Amethyst's tone brooked no refusal. A second, deeper look proved the reader correct. She had been so dazzled by the light and wings that she failed to look at the body under them. It was a warrior's body. A human warrior—strong and fierce.

"The only thing keeping you from being her, is that you can only see this." The image changed to show the woman Adriel had gotten used to seeing in the mirror. "Both images are truth. This woman has exactly the same potential as this," the fierce warrior was back.

"Okay, I think she's had enough." Gustavia moved from her seat to sling a protective arm around Adriel. "It probably feels like we're ganging up on her, and she's overwhelmed." To Adriel she said, "I can take you home, or if you want, you can stay the night with me. I've got the place to myself tonight with Finn out of town and Sam spending a week with her grandparents."

"I had to come here, did I tell you that?" Adriel said. "It was a compulsion that I couldn't ignore. I'd never ridden a bike before today. But I had to come. Why do you think that is? Fate? Estelle meddling to make sure you all were with me when she told me about Julius? It's been days since he disappeared. I find the timing suspicious, and it's just the kind of thing I would have done as a guardian if I needed to nudge a charge into being at the right place and time."

"You're saying she wanted you here because she knew we would offer to help. It's Julius, so there's no way we would let you go up against a threat to him alone. Fine. We've all been manipulated. So what. How we got here doesn't change anything. If Julius is in trouble, you can count me in." Kat said.

"He's my great-grandfather; you know I'm in." Julie looked at Gustavia who shouted, "Scoobies ride again."

"We have got to think of a better name." A wry comment from Amethyst.

Chapter Fourteen

Letting Pam know about her dinner with Callum proved to be Adriel's undoing. Not only was she forced to endure a second shopping trip, but this one included a session of hair and makeup.

"Is this really necessary? We're going to Athena's for pizza. It's just pizza. It's not a date."

Pulling dresses off the racks as she went, Pam marched down aisles filled with bright color and pattern. "It's a date with Longbrook's most eligible bachelor," she said, like it was a good thing.

"And why is that? Don't you think there's something wrong when a man his age has never married?" Following behind, Adriel returned all of Pam's choices to the racks for being too short or too bright.

Pam tossed a withering look over her shoulder, "He has been waiting for the right woman," she insisted.

"I can promise you I'm not her." At the end of the aisle, Adriel's empty hands earned her a long-suffering sigh. "Why don't you go out with him if he's so wonderful?" She tossed the comment off lightly; was unprepared for the pain she saw slide across Pam's features.

"He never asked me," a twist of the lips accompanied the muttered admission, "every other woman in town, but never me."

Figuring it might take days to get the taste of shoe out of her mouth, Adriel wasn't sure what to say. "He remembers fondly."

"What's that supposed to mean?" Pam said—hands on hips, hot color in her face.

That foot wasn't coming out of her mouth without surgical intervention now. Adriel spent a moment trying to find the right words. She held up both hands in surrender. "Nothing bad, I swear. Right after they found Ben he stopped by to...well, I don't know why he stopped by, but he seemed to need to talk about the past. It was a short conversation and he only mentioned—in passing—how he felt sorry for you and that you had guts."

"Lovely. I have other," Pam glanced down, "*attributes*. All he sees are my guts. I don't know what's worse, that he hasn't noticed them or that he pities me."

"You're looking at this the wrong way. I've known plenty of Lotharios in my time. None of them respected their conquests. Callum respects you."

"This is a weird conversation to have about the man you're going out on a date with tonight."

"It's not a date. Is there another way I can say it so it sinks in?"

Pam shrugged off the truth, along with regrets about her non-relationship with Callum, and got right back on the giddy train.

"Look at these wedges, they'd go perfect with that little strappy number."

"The one so tight I'd have to unzip it to breathe? You remember where I came from, right? I might not even be allowed to date. There are probably rules. For all I know, a bolt of lightning could blast Athena's off the map."

"I hope not; they make the best calzone in three counties. Besides, it's just a date, nobody said you have to go to bed with him."

No amount of argument swayed Pam from her chosen course of action. Pizza was more of a date than she'd had in years, and she planned to live vicariously whether Adriel liked it or not. Although, with the stigma of Ben's death lifted, she might just say yes the next time Paul the delivery guy asked her out. For now, though, Adriel was getting a new hairstyle, and if there was a second opening at the salon, Pam might hedge her bets with Paul and try something new, too. Highlights might be nice.

In the end, Adriel left the salon looking only subtly different. A scant layer of red decorated the salon floor—just enough to remove split ends and thin back some of the bulk. Her head felt lighter, though, which wasn't the worst thing. Pam, however, walked out looking like a new woman in a sleek bob with an underlay of royal blue highlights that peeked through when she shook her head.

Buyer's remorse set in before they made it back to the Jeep. "It's too much, isn't it? I'm not a teenager. What will people think?"

Adriel placed a hand on Pam's arm, exerted enough pressure to stop her forward motion. "Does it really matter what people think? How does it make you feel?"

"Bold. It makes me feel bold."

"Then be bold."

"But what about vanity; isn't it one of the deadly sins?"

Adriel waited until they were seated in the Jeep to answer.

"Have you ever seen a sunset?" She asked.

"Of course."

"What about a field of daisies? Or a perfect white cloud in a perfect blue sky? A butterfly? A kitten?"

Pam nodded. "Then what makes you think a creator who would go to the trouble to make so many beautiful things would condemn you for doing the same?"

"When you put it like that..." Pam grinned and shook her head. "I really do love it."

***

Callum McCord sat on Adriel's front porch and watched the Jeep pull in. Sure, he was a little early, but she was also a

165

little late. He looked forward to teasing her about it just to see what that quick tongue of hers would fire back at him. He liked a woman with spunk.

Ignoring Adriel for the time being, he carefully levered himself out of the plastic lawn chair, taking care to keep the spindly legs from folding under the stress. The last thing he wanted to do was land in a sprawl on the porch floor. There was no coming back from something like that. He made his way to the driver's side to say hello to Pam Allen. He owed her a word of sympathy about Ben anyway.

He wasn't prepared for the new and improved version he saw when the tinted window slid down. Years of stress and worry were gone from a face he remembered was only a couple years older than his own. *This must be what closure looks like*, the thought.

"I came over here to ask you something, but now all I can think of is how lovely you look."

"You like it?" Pam blushed and gave her head a little toss to show the blue base underneath."

"I do. It suits you."

***

Adriel watched the exchange with interest. As much as he liked sparring with her, she could see Callum had a soft spot for Pam. Maybe a little push in her direction would bear fruit. No matter what Pam wanted to believe, Adriel had no interest in dating the man. She'd make sure he was aware of it before the night was over.

"I was thinking we could walk, if you don't mind. The weatherman says it's going to be a supermoon tonight."

"Like with a cape and tights?" Supermoon was a term Adriel had never heard.

"No, like when the full moon is at or near perigee or apogee so it looks bigger and brighter than normal."

166

"Ah, I see." Adriel did a quick calculation in her head, "so roughly every seven months."

"Sure." His information came from the TV weatherman; he couldn't have spelled perigee if his life depended on it. "Some people would find it romantic."

"And some people eat crickets. There's no accounting for taste." Nevertheless, she let him lead her toward town and Athena's. His mind might be on romance; she would keep hers on ham and pineapple pizza.

"Tell me about it. We could have gone anywhere. You're a cheap date."

"You asked for a conversation over dinner. That's all this is." She pushed the door open without waiting for him to do the gentlemanly thing. Over her shoulder, she tossed an airy, "I don't date."

"I do."

"Well, that will be one of the things you do alone tonight."

"Ouch." He mimed, getting an arrow to the chest. "That's cold." He followed her inside where he surprised her by ordering a twelve-inch meatless. Adriel stuck to her choice of pineapple and ham, but in the six inch size normally reserved for kids. The half hour they waited for their pizza was spent with him asking her a series of questions to which she had no believable answers. Adriel found it difficult to concentrate on skirting his questions about her past—too many things whirled around in her head.

When her patience ran out, she skewered him, "Why are you so intent on this being a date? I'd like to be friends with you, but nothing romantic can ever happen between us. I'm not looking for that in my life." For so many reasons; none of which he would understand.

"I'm drawn to you, Angel. I can't explain it. It's just chemistry."

"Callum, you need to put the test tubes back in their holders, because I'm not feeling it. I'm sorry. I think I need to leave now."

"No, please. I'll stop, I promise. Look, can I tell you something? Something private? And you'll never tell another person?"

"You have my word."

Callum leaned toward her, "I've got this reputation around town for being a lady's man." Athena's had filled up with people. Callum pitched his voice low enough so no one else would hear. "You're gorgeous and new in town, so my buddies expect me to, you know—bag you."

"Bag me?" A raised eyebrow accompanied her similarly low tone. For once, she got the gist of the slang. "That's...well, it's...the most disrespectful thing anyone has ever said to me."

"I know." Callum dragged a hand through his hair. "I'm sorry. I really do like you, though. It's not all about my reputation."

"I'm about to do you a favor, then." Adriel popped the last bite of pizza into her mouth.

"You're going to pretend this is a date so I can save face?" Callum grinned in anticipation—a fake was better than no date at all.

"Not even close." Adriel raised her voice to make sure everyone in the place could hear, "I'm sorry if you thought this was more than a meal between friends, but you're not my type. I don't go for shallow men who spend more time thinking with what's in their pants than what's in their head. So do yourself a favor and leave me alone." Adriel sailed out the door.

A red-faced Callum caught up with her halfway to the cabin, "Was that absolutely necessary?"

"Yes, it was. You are a forty-year-old man with a lot to give to the right woman. I'm not that woman, but I figured I'd do you both a favor and take your reputation off the table so you can finally grow up. Pam deserves so much more than a shallow playboy."

"Pam? I don't even...what?" Surprise stopped him in his tracks.

"I saw how you looked at her today, and did you know you smile every time you talk about her?" Her eyes searched his face, and what she saw brought on a chuckle. "I'm sorry, my mistake. You aren't a shallow playboy; you're just in denial, and maybe a bit socially inept." It takes one to know one, she thought.

She left him standing there with a dazed look on his face.

Chapter Fifteen

f anyone drove by, they might wonder why three full-grown adults were seated in a circle on a patch of grass near a newly dug ditch. None of them would see the figure of the boy sitting cross-legged in the center of the circle.

Adriel hated to put him through this, but there was no way around it. If she was going to help him move on, she had to help Zack solve Ben's disappearance. Ben's description of his death sounded like an accident followed by a panicked driver hiding the body to cover up the crime. Zack needed to hear the details first hand. BTF—before the fall—opening a channel between them would have been child's play. Now, the only way was a circuitous route involving Kat.

Finding Ben's killer was the key to sending him home to be with his family. If there was anything useful in his memory, they needed to find it.

"Do you trust me, Ben? I know we've only just met, and you've been alone for a very long time."

"Sure. You're a nice person. I can tell."

What she had to do next might change his mind. First, she introduced Kat.

"Hello, Ben. It's nice to meet you," Kat greeted him. "This is my husband, Zack. He's the police officer in charge of finding out who hurt you."

"He can't see me, can he?" Ben waved a hand in front of Zack's face.

171

Suppressing a smile, Kat replied, "No, but we're going to see if we can fix that."

"Is Adriel going to use her wings?" He turned to Adriel, "Are you? Can I touch them?"

The question floored her. "You can see my wings?"

"Well, sure. Can't you?"

If only I could, Adriel thought. "You can try." She exchanged a slightly panicked look with Kat, who squeezed her hand in support.

"Oh, boy. You're the best, Adriel." Ben scrambled closer, stretched out his hand while she waited to see what would happen next. Adriel's eyes widened when she felt him make contact.

Ben sighed. He stroked a single finger down the leading edge of a phantom only he could see. "Thank you," he turned shining eyes on Adriel.

"Um, guys? This is weird," Zack should have been used to weird by now, but sometimes it just sneaked up on him. "I saw a flicker."

Okay, Adriel thought, that makes this easier. "Did you see anything?" She asked Kat.

"Ben, can you do that again? If it's okay with Adriel." Kat shot her a questioning look.

"Of course. Ben, go ahead." Eagerly, he laid his whole hand against the living softness.

"I can see him," Zack involuntarily reached out, then snatched his hand back when it passed through what looked like solid flesh and bone. Right hand still resting in Adriel's, Kat couldn't resist the temptation to try. It was a tossup between who looked more surprised when her questing fingers brushed the silky hair back from Ben's face. So many years had passed since he'd felt the simple touch of another, he leaned into the brief contact.

In surprise, Kat dropped Adriel's hand with the intention of pulling Ben into the hug she sensed he craved. She got the second shock in as many minutes when her hands passed right through him.

"Zack, could you touch Adriel and then try to touch Ben's shoulder? Is it okay with you, Ben? Don't let go of Adriel's wing."

"Sure."

Zack did as Kat asked, and when his hand touched striped cotton, he yanked it back like it was burned. "Whoa. Adriel, how are you doing this?"

"I'm not. Maybe we'd better get on with this, because I don't know how long it will last."

Zack took Ben through all the same questions Adriel had already asked. A few minutes of gentle probing satisfied Zack he had drawn out every nuance. He nodded to Adriel. It was time to take it up another level.

"How are you feeling, Ben?" Adriel searched him for signs of stress. Seeing none, she continued, "I need you to let Kat look inside your memories for clues to who might have hurt you."

"Didn't never see him. Just the car."

"I know. Since we found your…"

"You mean my bones?"

Instead of trepidation and fear, his expression was one of keen interest.

"Yes. That's exactly what I mean."

"It's like a Hardy Boys mystery. The case of the missing something or other. What do I have to do?"

"Let Kat look inside your memories."

"Like mind reader stuff? Neato keen. Will it hurt?" A little fear now, but mostly excitement.

"No. While she's looking, I'll try to protect you from seeing anything scary. All you have to do think about something you really love. Just concentrate on one thing and we'll do the rest."

"Okay. I'm ready." He scrunched up his face in concentration and Adriel couldn't help but smile at his enthusiasm.

Kat opened the connection while Adriel stood as shield. Both were able to see his memories: Pam as a young girl,

173

without the pall of grief, figured highly in his mental playback. His parents, a day at the fair, the scratchy tongue of a kitten licking his face, the first day of school, learning to ride a bike—these were the highlights of a young life cut way too short. The simple joy he had lived within was so strong and so deep.

Working forward to the time of his death, Adriel did her best to shield him from the sights and sounds. The thunk of the car, any pain he might have felt she took into herself. He'd been completely honest with her about not having seen his killer, but there were clues he was too young to comprehend.

Leaving the shields in place, Adriel watched as Kat pulled back, and then slowly withdrew.

"Ben, it's okay, you can relax now. It's all over."

"You're done? Nothing happened." He sounded relieved and disappointed at the same time. "Did it help?"

"Yes, we know where to begin now." Maintaining contact with Adriel, Kat pulled Ben into a one-armed hug. "Thank you for talking to us."

Ben turned his head toward the road. "Someone's coming."

She glanced in the direction he was looking and saw Callum strolling toward them. Out of the corner of her mouth Adriel said, "He looks upset."

Ben flashed a cheeky grin. "Right. See you later, Alligator."

He was gone. Alligator? Mortals say the strangest things.

To Kat and Zack, Adriel said, "I'll meet you inside. This won't take long." She got a look at the speculation on Kat's face, "It's not what you think."

***

Callum barely noticed Zack and Kat as they walked past him to enter the cabin. His focus was squarely on Adriel, who rose from the grass and walked to meet him.

"Do you have any idea what you've done?" Hot anger sparked the air around him.

"Not really." Her lips twitched. Of course she did.

"I can't stop thinking about Pam, and it's all your fault." In the way his hand rose then fell, Adriel read the urge to poke her. She let the grin slide over her face, then let it widen when he squinted at her. "Are you some kind of witch? I feel like someone cast a spell on me."

"All I did was pull your head out of your..." The squint was joined by a raised eyebrow, "...pants. What did you think I was going to say?"

"Never mind that. What am I supposed to do now?"

"I don't know. Turn on that lady-killer charm you bragged about. Or better yet, for once in your life, be honest with her and with yourself. Tell her how you feel. Ask the woman out to dinner. You might have to convince her your intentions are good." Adriel paused, "They are good, right. She's not going to be another notch on your lady-killer gun."

His snort at the visual eased the tension. "No, my intentions are honorable. I knew the moment I met you my life was about to be turned upside-down, I just never thought it would be like this." Callum reached for Adriel, planted a smacking kiss on her lips and walked back the way he had come.

***

"I saw that," Kat singsonged when the screen door slammed behind Adriel.

"Get your mind out of the gutter. It was a thank you kiss for putting his feet on the path to the right woman. Nothing more. I'd rather talk about what happened with Ben. Did you bring Zack up to speed?"

"She did. It was an accident; no doubt in my mind. Ben was late going home, so dusk had already fallen. He moved over into the grassy verge, but not as far as he thought. The

175

headlight blinded him when he looked back, and he swerved at just the wrong time. Does that fit with your impressions?"

"Completely. The first time Ben looked back, the driver was over the line, then right before the impact, the car was too far to the right. It looked like he or she overcompensated." Adriel replayed the scene in her head. Something about what Ben had witnessed triggered a niggle in the back of her mind, but the more she tried to bring it clear, the more it slid away.

"Based on the trajectory, it looked like the driver was impaired. Maybe by age or alcohol," Kat added while Adriel nodded her agreement.

"I think we can eliminate age," Zack mused, "or maybe not. I'm still fuzzy on how the details work when it comes to ghosts. Let's say Ben didn't cross over because he couldn't until his killer was found. If the killer was an elderly person thirty years ago, they would be long dead by now. Wouldn't their death satisfy Ben's unfinished business?"

"It's a tough call. There are three possible motivations connected to his journey. Finding the body, identifying the killer, and getting justice. Usually those last two happen together, but not always. It's not the first, since his bones were found and he's still here. The killer's own death would usually satisfy both of the other two, but not always."

Kat picked up where Adriel left off, "Let's say someone else knew or strongly suspected where Ben's body was buried. If that person keeps the secret, they become complicit, and Ben's unfinished business transfers to them. I don't think that's what's happening here, though."

"Nor do I." Adriel said. "That scenario is usually reserved for people who know exactly who killed them and who is keeping the secret. Ben has no idea. I'm leaning toward his killer still being alive."

"A drunk driver makes the most sense given the lengths taken to hide the body. There's a good chance it was a habitual offender. I'll pull driving records for DUI violations over the past thirty years. It's a place to start.

Chapter Sixteen

"Are you doing anything tonight?" Turning to avoid slamming into Hamlin while the three of them unloaded the food truck, Adriel tossed the question at Pam.

"Let's see, there's my dinner with the queen, I can't put that off again. Then later I was thinking of rearranging my video collection. They've been in alphabetical order for so long, I'm thinking I might change it up and create a complex rating system based on seven points of likability to sort them by."

"Is that supposed to be humor? We don't do corny where I come from."

"Ouch, burn," Hamlin teased Pam.

"Burn? That was barely even warm." Her smile was, though. After only seeing the occasional glimpse of this side of Pam over the years, Hamlin enjoyed her lighthearted laughter.

"I'd like you to meet some friends of mine."

Pam wanted to ask a bajillion questions, but with Hamlin in close proximity, settled for saying yes. Even worse, there was no chance over the rest of the day to get Adriel alone and grill her for information.

So, when she arrived at the cabin after work, Pam had no idea what she was walking into. The mid-sized SUV in the yard suggested Adriel probably wasn't entertaining angels. Or ghosts. Too bad. That might have been fun.

The sound of female voices raised in laughter intimidated Pam enough to halt her forward progress. All through her teenage years, when other girls grouped into cliques, none included the awkward subject of speculation who wouldn't have put herself forward in any case. Experience insisted this would be no different. She had turned to leave when Adriel stepped onto the porch.

"Pam? Were you leaving? Come inside and meet my friends. Please?" Adriel's tone soothed away doubt, but not the hesitation making Pam stay a few steps behind. She had no idea what to expect, outside of being the weird one in the group.

"Ladies, I'd like you to meet Pam. She's my boss and landlord. More importantly, she's my friend." Too dumbfounded to speak coherently, Pam stammered out a perfunctory greeting. She tried not to stare, she really did, but Gustavia in full regalia was a sight worth a good, long look. And it wasn't even one of her crazier getups. She'd taken a page out of Amethyst's book and gone for a monochromatic color palette. She wore gladiator sandals laced almost to the knee in a deep blue shading toward green. An A-line skirt, a Gustavia original, swung just below the knee—much shorter than her typical ankle dusters. Pam thought the material had been constructed from patchwork strips of old shirts—all different patterns in shades of tropical blues. A closer look revealed both pockets and buttons scattered at random intervals. A teal colored tank in shiny material topped by only five or six strings of beads completed the outfit. Into her hair, Gustavia had braided a collection of feathers and a handful miniature plastic flamingos.

Next to her, Amethyst's floaty fairy dress with yards of diaphanous chiffon in a deep purple that exactly matched her lipstick, came off as rather tame. At least the other two women looked normal. Maybe, for once, Pam wouldn't be considered the oddball.

"Pam, this is Julie Hayward-Kingsley. She's an up-and-coming photographer. And then we have Gustavia, who is an author of children's books. That vision in purple next to her is Amethyst Grayson. You'll have to ask her to read your aura." Amethyst gave Adriel a nod. "And last but not least, this is Kat Canton. Incidentally, Gustavia is Zack Roman's sister, and Kat is his girlfriend."

Before Adriel could provide Kat's occupation, Pam pointed a finger at her. "I've heard of you. You're the medium who works with Zack sometimes. I had no idea Adriel traveled in such illustrious circles." Smiles and warm greetings proved a perfect remedy for Pam's remaining shyness.

"Come, eat dinner with us, and we'll tell you how we came to be friends. It's a story worth writing a book about. We're having...what did you call it, Julie? Potluck? I'm not sure what that is exactly."

"It just means we all brought food with us. I made my famous eggplant lasagna. Gustavia raided her vegetable garden for salad fixings. Kat brought marinated chicken, and we talked Amethyst into making a batch of those cookies we all love. They're full of nuts and seeds and hunks of white chocolate."

Pam's eyes lit up. This was another way she could fit in. "Hang on one sec. I need to go out to my car." She returned with Adriel's favorite: a loaf of Hamlin's delicious French bread—fully two feet long, and full of crusty goodness. "This should go nicely with the meal."

By the end of dinner, Pam felt like one of the group. She'd made them recount parts of the story twice. "If I wasn't in the middle of my own fantastic tale, I'd be calling around to see if there was a rubber room missing its occupants."

"I think this is the first time we've been able to tell the whole story straight out to anyone. Even my folks don't know parts of what happened. Speaking of family, Adriel filled us in about your brother. I hope you won't think we're butting in, but we want to help." Kat glanced at Adriel for confirmation and waited for Pam's response, which came in the form of tears.

"You're all so nice. I'm sorry I'm being so emotional. It's just everything happened so quickly. But, for the first time in a long time, I don't feel like I'm all alone."

"Then I think I should tell you I've already had the pleasure of meeting Ben." Kat's smile widened at the memory of his sweet face. She went on to help Adriel describe the visit. "From the information he provided, Zack thinks we're looking for a drunk driver."

"Oh." A pause then, "Oh, Adriel. Do you remember me telling you about Bill and the fishing trip? Do you think it could have been him or one of his friends? Kat, tell Zack to look at William Dooley, Damien Oliver, and Graham Brier. Although, if Adriel's right and Lydia's death has anything to do with Ben's, that would eliminate Graham since he's been living on the other side of the country for years, and I would have heard if he had come back for a visit."

"Assuming the killer also sabotaged the ditch digging equipment, it probably wasn't Damien. Remember he mentioned how adding sand to the fuel tank wasn't the best way to put a vehicle out of commission for an extended period."

Pam frowned. "I can't picture Bill being cold-hearted enough to leave my brother in an unmarked grave all these years, but he's the only one left. Unless it was some stranger passing through, and everything else was just a series of coincidences."

Chapter Seventeen

"I'm telling you, it wasn't me. I may be a washed up loser, but I'm no killer." Bill looked Pam right in the eye.

"Then why all the fuss about the ditch? What do you care?"

Bill lowered his voice. "A friend called in a favor."

"Who?"

"Doesn't matter. I just did what I was told."

"It matters. Lydia Keough may have died to stop anyone finding those bones. I see you hadn't thought of that." Adriel said to a shocked Bill.

"It was Edward, okay? Edward wanted the protest."

It was the last name Adriel expected to hear. Edward could have stopped the construction before it started.

"But you do have a secret." Adriel made it a statement, not a question. She took a shot in the dark. "Does it have something to do with dancing pants?" His might have been one of the voices from the parking garage.

Pam's elbow jabbed Adriel hard in the ribs. Based on the color draining from Bill's face, though, she'd hit pay dirt.

"How did you find out about that?" Panic put him on the hairy edge of the fight or flight response. With his bum hip, he wasn't going to get far. A look at Adriel and he knew she could take him in a fight. There was nothing for it but to give in and reveal what he had kept hidden for thirty years.

"I cheated on Rosa the weekend Ben was killed. It was a stupid thing to do and I felt horrible about it after. An older girl took an interest in me and my brains fell into my pants. When I sobered up, I realized I couldn't face Rosa, so I did what any idiot would do. Got drunk again and took off to join the rodeo." Unsaid words hung in the air. "Damien and Graham got into a fight over nothing, and the fishing trip broke up early, so I left when the others did. One look at my sweet Rosa's face and I couldn't live with myself. I was up in the stands at the fairgrounds with a six pack, trying to drink myself to death when the rodeo started. The rest is history, or town gossip. Whichever. When I came back a year later, Rosa forgave me and we got married."

"And you're sure you never saw anyone driving erratically that night? How did you get back from the lake?"

"No one but me, but I stayed off the main roads. Dirt bike. I took the old logging trail down past Hamm Bog. Had a near miss with a moose."

"Can you remember what Damien and Graham were fighting about?" Damien was the other name on their suspect list."

Bill took a minute to think about it. "Probably nothing. Just a group of stupid kids thinking we were big shots up there on our own with a case of beer we paid for ourselves. Graham used to get mean when he drank."

"None of you were over eighteen. Who bought the beer for you."

A shutter dropped over Bill's face. "He can't tell you anything, so there's no sense digging in that manure pile. Besides, your family has been through enough. Pam, you've known me all our lives. Do you really think I could stand by and watch you suffer if I knew something that would ease your pain?"

"Please, Bill. I need to know." Pam rested her hand on his. The name he spoke came as a complete shock.

"Craig."

"My uncle? He couldn't have had anything to do with Ben's death."

"I should hope not." Bill pulled out his wallet to pay for the coffee and donuts.

"Put your wallet away. This one's on me." *Probably the last food he'll ever eat here*, she thought.

***

Three times Adriel circled back to the beginning of the maze in Craig's mind. All of the signposts she put there last time had been moved. Wily rascal. Well, he wasn't the only fox in the woods. The second she closed her eyes to run through the gauntlet mentally, it clicked. On vastly different scales, Craig's mind and his house were laid out in a similar pattern. That was the key to the whole thing. She had the how; it was time to figure out the what. The secret lay in one of the countless boxes of seemingly random items. Presumably the dirty socks and plastic cutlery could be ruled out. Also hats, cookbooks, empty cans, labels and lids. What items had he taken the most care with? The well-wrapped acorns? Worth a shot.

"Are you sure this isn't a total waste of time?" Estelle's patience was shorter than an eyelash these days. With Julius missing and the only hope of finding him resting on the return of Adriel to full angel-level powers, Adriel took the brunt of Estelle's ire.

"Back off, trainee. I'm doing the best I can."

"I'm sorry. You know it's the situation, not you. This feels off."

"If you have a better idea, I'm open to it. Bill implicated Craig. We already know Craig has something hidden in here, we just need to find it."

Adriel closed her eyes to get a better mental image of the cabin. A right then two lefts and another right should do it. Turning the corner to find Craig standing there looking sad clinched her hunch, and proved she was on the right track. "You're here to drag my secret shame out into the light where I have to look at it."

"No, Craig. You don't have to look." After talking to Bill, she and Pam agreed Craig couldn't face his part in the events leading up to his nephew's hit-and-run death. In his grief, he had locked away the memory and created this complicated mental structure to protect it. A maze of living walls designed to contain the thing he needed to not see. He held a piece of the puzzle and Adriel needed to see how it fit. "I can shield you if that's what you need me to do, and you never have to know what I found."

Thirty years of hiding the truth had led him to this point; facing it now might set him free, or it might take what sanity he had left. Adriel tugged on the silver cord that bound her to Estelle. Who knew what might happen once she poked this hornet's nest. Craig could freak out and change the pathways, leaving her stranded.

Adriel took Craig's silence to mean she should move on by herself. Brushing past him where he stood, she missed his stricken expression and the subtle but steady drop in temperature. She reached for the door handle, which felt odd under her hand. Bone. The door handle was made from bone. Creepy. A shiver raised the hair on her arms, but she twisted it open anyway to reveal a vast and empty cavern. Adriel refused to accept defeat.

A single step into the room caused the silver rope to tug painfully against her middle. Adriel might have tried to push the issue, but a rapidly thickening mist rose to bar her way.

Between one breath and the next, chaos erupted. A shriek tore the air, the sound powerful enough to push Adriel back a step, then another, until she stood right next to Craig. A whimper escaped his lips, pierced through the inhuman scream. Whipping her head around, Adriel saw the terror on Craig's face and the notebook clutched in his hand.

She'd been wrong this whole time. It wasn't a memory trapping Craig in his head. The stench of brimstone slammed into her like a wall.

"Galmadriel, look out." Estelle's shout came a second too late.

Darkness fell over Adriel like a wave, sucked her under, rolled her as though she weighed nothing. The cord binding Adriel snapped; the force of it breaking catapulted Estelle out of Craig's mind, which snapped shut behind her and would not reopen.

Adriel was trapped, Julius was missing. Estelle could only think of one thing to do.

***

"It just makes sense. Ammie's booked solid these days, which leaves Reid stuck in the bedroom if he's home. If we turn this place into a storefront of sorts, we could offer package deals. More than half of my regular clients are hers already. Unless you've changed your mind about living together?" Kat speared a shrimp off Zack's plate and popped it in her mouth.

"Never. We could make it official if you'd just say yes."

She waved her fork at him. "Not until you've had a chance to see what being married to me would be like. It's more of a commitment than you think."

Zack rolled his eyes like he did every time she tried to make the point. "You sleep at my place four nights a week as it is. What's going to be different on the other three?"

"I have my..." Kat's eyes rolled back in her head.

Heart hammering, Zack lunged to her side.

"Adriel is in trouble. Come. Now." Estelle's voice boomed from Kat's lips, giving Zack an involuntary shiver. That kind of thing didn't happen often, but he wasn't sure he'd ever get used to it. When her eyes snapped open, she was just Kat again.

"We have to go. Hurry. Estelle showed me where they are. No lights or sirens, though. I'll call Ammie on the way. Julie and Gustavia, too."

185

By the time all four women and Zack assembled in Craig's room, twenty minutes had passed.

"They're both caught in his mind and I can't get in."

"That's because they're not in there alone." Amethyst turned her reading ability up to full force. "There's darkness in him. Why didn't you call me before she went in there? I could have kept this from happening."

"We didn't know. Adriel thought it was just one of Craig's memories haunting him. She wasn't expecting this. We have to help her, but I'm not sure how. I'm the worst guardian angel ever."

Gesturing for quiet, Amethyst turned to Kat. "What do you see?"

"The darkness is seeping into her. It's evil, but it doesn't feel like Billy did. Probably not an Earthwalker. If I use you as a…"

"Shield." Amethyst finished for her. "That's what I was thinking. We'll go in through Adriel and I'll heal her aura as we go. I can cast it out ahead like a shield while you watch for them. Estelle, can you bind us to you like you did Adriel?"

"I can, but that thing snapped my cord like it was rotten thread."

"What about this?" Gustavia cut in, "Have Estelle add Julie and me to the mix. She can anchor the cord around us like mountain climbers do when they need a second safety. Wrap it double and we'll help her pay it out as you go."

Estelle was already shaking her head, "I can't put you all at risk. There has to be another way."

"I want to help. Adriel is my friend, too. Do it. We're wasting time here," Julie squared off against her grandmother the angel. "Do it," she repeated. Estelle wasted no more time.

"Go. Go. We've got you," Gustavia reached for Julie's hand, and for Estelle's, thinking physical proximity would strengthen the bond. Light flowed along the silver binding to strengthen Amethyst's power.

Before the force of their combined will, the thing of darkness slowly fell back. Amethyst could feel it tasting her power just as surely as she measured the force mounted against her. Thinking it wise to keep a measure of her ability in reserve, she toned it down several notches. Just enough to meet strength with strength. With Kat directing her, she pushed slowly ahead, ignoring everything but her shield and the evil beyond.

"Do you hear it?" Kat whispered to Amethyst.

"No, what?"

"It's talking to me. Telling me to give up, that we can never defeat it. It's showing me images of Adriel and Julius being pulled screaming into the black."

"Fake. It's just trying to psych you out. Keep going." They stepped into Craig's mind. Into bedlam. Walls tumbled to rubble made walking difficult until Kat realized the pieces she was stepping over were more than bits of debris. "Ammie, stop a minute. Look. We're walking over pieces of his memories. See." Kat sifted through the debris for sections that matched.

"Give those to me." With nothing more than her touch, Amethyst healed the two shards together. Light flared to eat another piece of darkness. "Okay, I know what to do. Get down, now." Pushing Kat to the floor, Amethyst followed her, dropping the shield at the same time. She plunged her hands into the pile of debris and set the intention to heal firmly in her heart, mind, and soul.

Out from her hands, the light spread like a mist flowing over the ground. Everywhere it touched, fractured memories knit together to produce their own light—a flare that ate the screaming darkness right up to the source where it stopped. Silence fell like a curtain. Its weight pressed down on Kat so hard she had to struggle to turn her eyes toward where Amethyst's were already riveted.

***

Adriel pushed Craig toward where Amethyst and Kat huddled. When the light washed over her, it had brought something with it. The sure knowledge that in this place, she was no longer bound by flesh. No longer blocked.

She was the angel Galmadriel.

Head bowed as though in prayer, she let the light, the power, the fury of it flow through her in all its glory and grace. Wings of white so pure it dazzled the eye unfolded behind her, fanning once, then twice before stretching to their full span. More light flowed from her skin; beamed from her eyes as she turned them on the dark thing before her.

"Earthwalker, stand to face me."

Kat's whispered, "She's back," carried across the space to bring a short, but fierce smile.

"By my command, you will face me."

The figure that had been crouched before her slowly pulled himself upright. Wings as black as night unfurled—their span not quite a match for hers, but close. When his head lifted, Galmadriel's gasp echoed across the space.

"Malachiel."

He stood defiant before her. "Even when you fall, you shine," he spat the words at her.

"How did you come to me as a being of light if you are not of the grace?"

"It's easy to fool humans."

Amethyst muttered, "But it's not nice to fool Mother Nature." Galmadriel quelled her with a sideways glance.

"That was your mistake, Mal. I'm not human, and I'm not fallen. I'm earthbound." The words fell with the knell of truth. "This man is under my protection. You will not touch him again. Like you once said to me, stay away from what's mine."

Seething fury burned on his face.

"Go," Galmadriel roared, the force of her words hit him like a hurricane. In a swirl of dark fog, he was gone.

"Too easy." Kat hauled herself up to standing. "In the movies the bad guy always seems gone, and then he swoops in for one last hurrah."

"He still has Julius. Does that count?"

Chapter Eighteen

Craig Allen thought he was dead. You wake up with two angels staring down at you, it's a natural conclusion. Anyone might be forgiven for thinking so. Especially with his memory of the day's events wiped clean.

"Am I dead? What happened?" On second thought, it felt like he was in his own bed.

"How do you feel?" He certainly looked better than he had earlier. His eyes were clear and he seemed anchored in the present.

"Good. I think. I have a lot of questions."

Estelle laid a hand on his forehead to put him back to sleep. There was no time to deal with his questions right now.

"Did you find what you needed?" Estelle hoped so. "I need to file a report on Malachiel. It breaks my heart to see one of our own like that. I'll be back later so we can sort out a plan of action for finding Julius." Estelle didn't say it out loud, but with Malachiel behind his abduction, he could be anywhere. Moreover, she had the feeling the search and rescue mission was going to fall to Adriel, which meant Estelle would be the only angel allowed to help.

As of her last briefing, contact with The Earthbound—as Galmadriel was coming to be known—was forbidden to anyone other than her guardians until her motives were settled to the satisfaction of the entire collective. Based on the way things were going in that quarter, Estelle's estimate on it happening was sometime between now and never.

***

"We need to go back to the cabin; I think I know who killed Ben and Lydia." Adriel announced to Zack after spending a bit of effort folding her tall frame into the back seat of Kat's subcompact and ending feeling like a pretzel. "I think Barbie is missing her daily driver." The acid comment brought a snort from Julie, who watched the debacle from the beside her. Amethyst and Gustavia would follow in her car.

"Do you have any proof?" Zack would be happy to arrest the culprit, so long as he had enough evidence to make the charges stick.

"Maybe, but I need to check on a couple of things first. Julie, can you call Pam and have her meet us there? I need to tell her about Craig, and she deserves to be there when her brother's killer is arrested."

And that was the last thing Adriel would say on the matter until everyone gathered at the cabin.

***

"I know who killed Ben and Lydia," Adriel returned from the bedroom brandishing a red spiral-bound notebook. "Here's what I think happened."

"Bill and his buddies helped Craig paint this place the week before their fishing trip, and he paid them with a case of beer. Bill mentioned that Damien and Graham got into a fight, and we also know Bill cheated on his girlfriend that weekend, which means there were five people at the lake and not four."

"Dun, dun, dun," Gustavia couldn't help herself.

"We ruled out Bill because he left on a dirt bike; Graham because if the two deaths are related, he has an ironclad alibi

190

for Lydia's; as does Levi, who is dead. That only leaves Damien." Pam said.

"And the fifth person; the one Bill fooled around with."

"But we have no idea who that is."

"Oh, I think we do. At first I thought Lydia was killed to stop the construction from moving forward and keep Ben's bones hidden, but only because someone sabotaged the equipment first. Something else happened that made me think those two things might not be related." Energy still elevated from the altercation with Malachiel, Adriel paced the small space. Every so often that energy pulsed to raise gooseflesh on arms, and prickle the necks of everyone in the room.

"I found Edward wandering around in the field a few nights after Lydia died, and he mentioned having been out there before. That made me wonder if he was the one who sabotaged the equipment. Later, Bill said Edward was the one behind the picketing, and that clinched it."

"I'm still confused," Zack said, "Why do you think Lydia was killed, then?"

"Lydia was the older woman Bill cheated with that night. Damien knew the bones were going to come to light, and he also knew Lydia would put it all together; and, unlike Bill and Craig, there was nothing he could do to silence her."

"How did he silence my uncle?" Pam demanded.

"He sold the car to Craig. It's been sitting in the shed back there this whole time." Adriel turned to Zack.

"Remember when Ben mentioned seeing a plane right before the car hit him? Wait until you get a look at the hood ornament. Several years ago—according to Craig's diary— Bill Dooley came by to borrow a harrow and saw the car. The diary didn't say exactly what, but something Bill said triggered Craig to start thinking back to that day."

Adriel went back to the bedroom and returned to toss another notebook on the table.

"His diary entries started going strange right after that. I think he figured out what happened to Ben, and the guilt over providing the beer got to him. He felt responsible and couldn't

191

face telling anyone what he knew, so he disassociated completely in order to hide the memory so he could live with the guilt."

All the pieces slotted into place but one.

"But why would Edward sabotage the equipment? He could have put the kibosh on this ditch before the work ever started."

"He told me he wanted a break from town business after his heart attack. I think he was deliberately trying to ruin his own reputation, along with Lydia's.\, so they could both retire."

"It all fits. Show me the car."

***

When it was all over, Zack reckoned Damien Oliver set a record for the fastest confession ever given in the county lockup. If she'd been present, Kat could have told him how Estelle and Ben standing in the corner might have had something to do with it. It seemed the touching-the-wing trick worked on Estelle just as well as it had on Adriel. The sight of his victim watching over the proceedings had a profound effect.

Two days later, Ben's bones were released, and Pam finally got the chance to lay her brother to rest with her parents. The whole town turned out, including a sheepish Rodeo Bill. Callum McCord never left Pam's side during the entire service—a fact that was commented on in hushed tones.

Chapter Nineteen

"Are you ready?" Adriel's gentle hand on Pam's arm shook a little. How was she supposed to get through this if the angel wasn't even ready for what was about to happen. Tears welling, Pam managed a quivering nod. The prospect of seeing Ben again brought up so many emotions; she wasn't sure she could handle it.

"Ben is going to touch my wing," Adriel explained yet again, then nodded to Ben, who buried his hand in the living softness. Eyes squeezed shut, Pam missed the moment when Ben shivered into visibility. Even so, some change in the atmosphere triggered her awareness.

"Open your eyes. Don't be afraid, I am right here with you." Adriel made her voice as soft and soothing as she could, then gave little Ben another nod.

"Hey, Sissy. You're not scared of me are you?"

At the sound of his voice, just like she remembered it, Pam's knees turned to mush. A rush of exultation rose up in her so strongly that Adriel couldn't see how a fragile human body could hold it without bursting.

"Bennie, is that really you?"

"I'm standing right here. Oh, are we playing hide and seek? Are you it?"

Pam's eyes flew open. "No Ben, please don't hide again." She hunkered down to bring herself to his level. He looked exactly as he had the last time she saws him. Dressed in jeans, sneakers and his favorite red jacket. A shock of pale blond hair fell across clear blue eyes that twinkled when he grinned at her.

"Boy, you sure got bigger."

With a wry smile, Pam nodded, "And older. I know I look different. Does that scare you?"

"No. You love me, nothing to be scared of. I watched you lots of times. I called and called, but you never answered because you couldn't see me."

"So you know you're a…"

"A ghost? Yeah. Adriel 'splained everything. She's nice. She told me 'bout how I stayed with you instead of going into the light, and that was okay for a while. But now it's time for me to go be with Mom and Dad." He scuffed his little Converse-clad toe back and forth across the floor. "And I helped her figure out what happened to me."

Tentatively, Pam reached out a hand as though to stroke his hair, then pulled it back and looked up at Adriel. Her longing to touch him ran deep and strong.

"It's okay, Pam. You've both been waiting so long."

When the silky strands of his hair threaded through his sister's fingers, hesitation turned to joy. Pam pulled Ben in to hug him so tightly he squirmed in her arms in order to remain in contact with Adriel's wing.

"Hey Sissy, take it easy. You're squooshing me."

"Oh, Bennie boy, I can't help it. I've missed you so much." Laughter and tears mixed in the bittersweet moment that healed a heart broken for such a long time. The look Pam gave Adriel spoke volumes as she mouthed, "Thank you."

Tears ran down Adriel's face in a human show of emotion. She was learning how cathartic it felt to cry sometimes.

Turning back to the small but sturdy form, Pam asked, "Do you know what happened to you?"

"I was riding my bike down past old man Tilden's place, you know?"

Pam nodded.

"When I got to Keough's, there was a car coming up behind me, so I moved over into the grass like Dad taught me and put on my brakes. Then I must have fell and bumped my head, because it hurt for a minute. Then the light came, and I went home."

Another weight lifted off Pam's chest. He'd felt no fear or pain.

"The light's back, Sissy. I think it's almost time to go. Adriel says Mum and Dad will be there when I go into the light, but I don't want to leave you all alone. Should I stay?"

The lump threatened to choke Pam's words but she managed to swallow past it and say, "No, it's time for you to go. I'll be fine. One more hug?" She gave him another squeeze and a kiss, then stood up, one hand over her mouth to stop the sobs, and another over her heart.

"Love you Bennie Boy."

Ben took a step backwards into the leading edge of the light. His figure shimmered for a moment, then elongated as he appeared to age rapidly. Where the boy had stood was now a man.

Pam gasped at this glimpse of what Ben could have become if he had lived. The same sweetness that had always marked him as a boy shone through the man as well. His eyes lingered on Pam with a hundred things left unsaid, and a reluctance to leave her.

"Love you, Sissy." His voice rang out with authority, "Be happy." He slid a hand off Adriel's wing, stepped back into the light, and was gone.

"There will never be words enough to thank you for the gift you just gave me," Pam pulled the still-sobbing Adriel into her arms. "Whether you ever figure out how to use those wings of yours again, you will always be the angel who saved me."

Chapter Twenty

Estelle shimmered into the empty spot next to where Adriel and Pam still embraced. A tear trembled on her lower lashes. Letting go of Adriel, Pam watched the place where Ben had stood for long minutes. She braced herself against this second loss—her shoulders slowly straightening. When she turned back, her expression held more peace than sorrow. Closure smoothed away the last of the grief lines to leave her face shining and smooth.

"I can't believe he's..." she broke off to tilt her head and gaze at Estelle. "Who's this?"

"She can see me?" Estelle panicked. "She shouldn't be able to do that."

"Side effect of touching Ben while he was touching me."

Pam listened to the exchange; her lips quirked slightly.

"Is it permanent? Am I going to lose points for this?" Estelle was nonplussed.

"There's a point system now?" Adriel didn't think she'd been gone long enough for there to have been changes of that magnitude.

"Figure of speech." Estelle qualified, while Pam's quirk turned to a full-out grin. "And answer the question."

"But first, could you introduce me to your friend?" Pam said.

"Sorry, this is Estelle. She's my trainee." It was the best word Adriel could find to describe the relationship given its outside the box—way outside—nature. "The effect is temporary. Your energy levels will return to normal, and you won't be able to see Estelle. It might take a few hours or even days."

Visible relief painted both faces with the same expression. Adriel concealed a small smile just before her head fell back and her eyes closed themselves tightly. Images of Pam's life to come played through her mind on fast-forward. With grief no longer clouding her life, Pam would stop holding back. There would be Callum, and love, and marriage, and even a child. It was a future filled with living, and not just existence. Ben would be proud to know his sister had found the will to move past his loss.

Estelle spoke directly into Adriel's mind, "You know you can't stay here, right?"

A sigh wafting past her lips, Adriel said, "I know. My work here is almost done." She looked around at the now clean and tidy cabin. Craig would return, soon, to live out his days in the only home he'd ever really known. At least she was not the one who would have to explain where his stash had gone. Hopefully, he no longer needed it, anyway.

The only thing left was to say her goodbyes.

The powers that be had other plans.

12718101R00106

Printed in Great Britain
by Amazon